BUILDING BABY BROTHER

STEVEN RADECKI

Cover design by Niki Lenhart
nikilen-designs.com

Published by Paper Angel Press
paperangelpress.com

ISBN 978-1-953469-32-8 (Trade Paperback)

10 9 8 7 6

FIRST EDITION

For my Josh,
and to the fine man that he's become

1

"**D**ad, can I have a baby brother?"

I paused, still holding the Lego piece in my hand.

"Are you sure you want one?" I tried to sound casual about it. "You know you'd have to help take care of him. He'd be in your toys …"

"I know, Dad."

Josh gave me an exasperated look. We'd been through all this before.

It wasn't that I necessarily wanted to deprive Josh of the sibling experience; I'd been through it myself. I also knew that it wasn't all play time and brotherly love.

"Okay, Josh," I said, turning to face him. "It's your choice: you can have a baby brother or too many toys."

Yeah, I admit it. It was kind of a cheap shot. But it was a whole lot easier than explaining the real reason.

Before answering, Josh took a quick look around his bedroom. He surveyed his collections of Lego sets, action figures, and the stacks of video game discs.

"Too many toys," he finally announced, nodding firmly in confirmation. With that decided, he turned his attention back to our current construction project, snapping a new piece into place.

Whew, I thought. *Dodged that bullet. Again.*

Later that night, after *finally* getting Josh to bed, I settled myself at my desk with the intent to pay the bills and deal with other household-related recordkeeping. Glancing at the clock, I saw that it was quite a bit later than I'd hoped. I considered putting off those tedious chores for just one more night, but knew there was no guarantee that tomorrow night would be any better than this one. The odds were that it was unlikely to be. It's amazing how many excuses, and other delaying tactics, young children will resort to rather than simply closing their eyes and going to sleep. It's probably not quite as astonishing, though, as when you look away for a moment, only to turn back to find their head against the pillow and their breathing steady and slow.

Might as well get it done, I encouraged myself, barely succeeding in fighting back a yawn. *Most of these people* do *like to get paid on time.*

It's strange, but when I'm working, I usually prefer it to be quiet. At night, though, and when tackling these kinds of tasks, I find a little background noise comforting — just something playing at low volume so I'd be able to hear Josh if he needed me.

I wasn't really in the mood for music, so I turned on the small television that sat on a low cabinet across from my desk. The screen lit up with a graphic and bloody scene from an episodic police procedural.

Ugh. I can catch the late news if I want to see that …

I changed the channel. Again. And then again.

Fairly quickly, I despaired of finding any programming that was not an overly gritty adult drama or a talk show host chatting about the latest geopolitical happenings with sparkling celebrities who had also dropped in to discuss their latest motion picture, television series, concert tour, stint in rehab, or any combination of the above.

My fingers paused on the remote control when I caught sight of a small doe-eyed boy moving through blue-tinged darkness across a moonlit hillside. I recognized it as a scene from Kubrick's last science fiction movie. While it wasn't among my favorites, neither was it among the worst, and I hadn't planned to really watch it anyway.

It might have been avoidance behavior, or simply fatigue, but my mind kept drifting when it was supposed to be keeping track of which payments I'd already made. I tried to focus on my balances due, but my eyes and attention kept wandering back to the images on the television screen. I watched the small artificial boy move along the scenery, and I began to wonder if it was really possible to create something like him.

Creating the software to do it; that I could almost imagine. That's my day job: I plan and develop computer programs. I try to make the hardware do what my clients want it to do, to produce the results that they want from it. I don't typically design or build the actual circuitry or components. I leave that to the electrical and mechanical engineers. I was certain that I could never construct a cybernetic being as complex as the ones presented in that film.

By the time I finally went to bed, though, I found that I was still thinking about it, unable to banish the notion from my thoughts. I tried telling myself that there were technological and financial realities to be consider — ones that would make such a project almost impossible for me to achieve alone.

After being unsuccessful in wholly silencing the persistent voice in my head, I finally decided that only thinking about the notion would cost me nothing. Well … other than perhaps the price of the loss of a little sleep or a few unusual dreams. So, I closed my eyes and let my mind see how far it could go with the idea.

It was still working the idea the next morning and, after I had dropped Josh off at school, I began to realize that not only might it be possible, but that it might also be practical, using only off-the-shelf components. With the large number of computer stores in the area, I thought it possible to get everything I might need. If I couldn't find it at the one of the many shops, I had several friends who worked for some of the major computer and chip companies. They could probably get their hands on whatever eIse I might need. I even began mentally composing a proposed shopping list: motherboards, memory, hard drives …

While I suffered from no delusions that what I might create would be anywhere near as complex as the one I'd seen in that movie — or from *any* movie, for that matter — I had, in the span of one evening, gone from "That's impossible!" to "How hard it could be?"

Well, a lot harder than I thought, it turned out. Much harder.

2

I'LL SPARE YOU THE DETAILS OF HOW I DID IT. It's not just that I need to keep much of it secret until the possible patent issues are resolved, but the details are probably only interesting to other computer scientists or electrical engineers. Some of them, I'm sure, would be quick to point out all of the things that I did wrong, or could have done better. The point is, though: *I did it.*

So, many weeks later, I waited impatiently for Josh to arrive home. His mother had taken him for the weekend, but had arranged to drop him off a day earlier than usual, as she was leaving on a business trip early the next morning. I hadn't complained; I don't think Josh minded either.

They were scheduled to arrive in the late afternoon, about an hour or so before dinner. Right then, it was only a little past noon. So, I paced. And I kept checking the clock. And then I began to mumble vague curses when they did not arrive at the expected time. Almost thirty minutes after that — although it seemed to me to be far longer — I heard a car pull up at the curb.

I greeted them at door, opening it while they were both still several steps away. Carolyn paused at the edge of the doorstep. Her eyes widened when she finally noticed me. Everything in her entire expression communicated her disapproval.

Although I hadn't looked in any mirrors, I had a pretty clear mental image of what I must have looked like. I'd spent the last few days driving myself on too little sleep and my only sources of nutrition having been food that could be quickly prepared in the microwave or consumed directly from its container. My face had not been closely acquainted with a razor in at least three days. I'm certain my eyes reflected the little sleep that I'd had. I knew, at least, that I didn't smell as bad as I probably looked. I'd showered — although I'd begrudged every moment that concession to hygiene and social politeness had taken away from me finishing the project before Josh arrived.

In some ways, it reminded me of the handful of all-nighters that I'd had pulled in college. The similarity, however, was nostalgic at best. I'd been much younger then. I knew I would pay dearly for this later — and probably for the next several days as well. One thing I learned as I've gotten older: the value of a good night's sleep should not be underrated.

Josh glanced up curiously, looking at me perhaps a moment longer than usual. He made no comment, though, as he then wheeled his small suitcase past me and into the house. He was rarely very chatty for the first few hours after he came back from spending time with his mother. Today seemed to be no different. I didn't mind, though, knowing the grand surprise that awaited him in the basement.

Carolyn waited expectantly on the doorstep. This was the awkward part. I was eager for Josh to see the results of my work, but I wasn't ready to show Carolyn — at least not yet. I couldn't simply dismiss her, though. So, I took a slow breath, hoping that it masked the sigh beneath it.

"Do you want to come inside for a minute?"

"Sure," she replied curtly, eyeing me one more time before stepping inside. I was sure that she was wondering whether the condition of the house matched my personal state.

I was actually surprised, for it was something she would have typically preferred not to do. That meant, I realized, that she needed to discuss something with me. Those conversations were seldom pleasant.

What she did first was to hand me a large envelope. The muscles in my neck and shoulders tightened into steel knots. We'd been trying to settle the final conditions of our divorce for months. I automatically assumed this was yet another in what seemed to be an unending stack of impenetrable legal documents that I needed to decipher in the hope that we might eventually reach a mutually tolerable agreement.

"Josh has a field trip next week," she said. "Here are the signed permission slips."

I accepted the envelope without looking at it. A few of those muscles relaxed.

"I also ordered some cookies," she murmured. She looked away as she said it, as if admitting that doing something charitable for Josh's school physically pained her.

Nodding dumbly, I made a mental note to do the same. A vague memory of Josh mentioning some kind of fund-raising activity before I'd dropped him off at school on Friday morning flickered through my mind.

She brushed past me without looking at me. A moment later, I heard the bathroom door close and its lock click.

I stared down at the envelope in my hand, trying to think of where to put it so I would remember to give it back to Josh on Monday morning before he left for school. While I was still considering that, he returned and gave me a quick, but sincere, hug.

"Hi, Dad."

I smiled down at him and then knelt so I could see him eye to eye. It struck me suddenly that I didn't need to lean down quite as far as I used to.

"Hey, kiddo. Have a good time?"

He shrugged.

That simple movement spoke volumes. As far as he was concerned, whatever they had done together had held very little of interest for him. Carolyn had probably been preoccupied with preparing for her trip, so had probably simply dragged him along on her errands. I wanted to be annoyed, but I was too tired, and too wired with anticipation, to summon up the necessary outrage.

"Well," I whispered to him while I worked up a renewed smile. I tried to keep it from growing too large, surprised at how much effort that required. "I have something to show you —"

"Is it a secret? Or are girls invited too?"

My eyes remained on Josh's face as my cheeks grew suddenly warm. I hadn't heard Carolyn return. Startled, I had to keep from toppling onto my knees.

It wasn't that I had intended to keep my little project a secret from her … exactly. I just hadn't envisioned her being there when I'd unveiled it for Josh.

"What do you think?" I asked him.

Josh shrugged again. "It's okay," he said. "I guess."

In my peripheral vision I could tell from her tight expression that she was not exactly pleased by his lack of enthusiasm. Still, I let it go. It was her issue, not mine, and I wasn't going to burden Josh with it. Not right then.

"Okay then," I replied, trying hard to sound genuinely enthusiastic, but I could not meet Carolyn's eyes. "Come with me."

I stood and offered my hand to Josh. He took it, gripping it firmly, and the three of us headed toward the basement.

I had dimmed the lights — mostly for dramatic effect. If they were peeking into the darkness, they wouldn't be able to see much. Covered with a dark sheet, illuminated only by shadowy reflected light, the object that lay on my workbench appeared only as a large, non-descript shape.

Both Josh and Carolyn walked toward it, moving cautiously in the darkness. I held up a hand to stop them before they touched anything.

"Wait a minute."

I turned the lights up and then went over to Josh. I knelt so that I was once again face-to-face with him.

"Josh?" I asked him. "Do you remember all those times you asked for a baby brother?"

"Yeah ..." he answered warily.

A smile spread across my face. His eyes followed me as I rose and strode over to the workbench. And then, with what was probably an overly dramatic flourish, I pulled the sheet away.

"Allow me to present Baby Brother 1.0!"

At first, Josh seemed to stare at it without understanding. Then, his eyes grew wide and lit up. I have to admit, so did my ego.

"Dad!" he exclaimed, his voice rising into a full shout. "This is so cool!"

He made a slow circuit around the perimeter of the workbench, studying everything he could about my creation without getting too close to it. I could tell, even though his radiant curiosity, that he remained a little uncertain. My gaze followed his as it swept over the still form.

I'd dressed it in some clothes that Josh had outgrown. They didn't fit it particularly well, but they did help it appear to be more real, even though closer inspection would immediately reveal otherwise. I did worry that putting clothing on it might lead to potentially embarrassing inquiries as to its anatomical correctness. If the question came up, though, the answer would be "No." There was no reason in the world that this particular creation needed to be "fully functional".

Its hair was artificial, created from an inexpensive wig that I'd purchased from a local costume shop. I hoped that it looked close enough to the real thing that you'd have to look twice to notice that it wasn't. I'd also given it eyebrows and eyelashes. That last feature, in particular, had taken me many more hours to get right than I ever would have imagined. I think I have a far better understanding now why it takes some women so long to get ready to go out.

Now its hands ... those were among my more inspired creations. I'd originally planned to just use thick latex gloves to cover their internal mechanisms, along with plans to create something more life-like at a later time. One day, though, I was out shopping — for what, I don't remember — and ran across a crate of Halloween merchandise on clearance at one of those everything-for-a-dollar discount stores.

There, stacked haphazardly among assorted other items intended to be either gruesome or disgusting, if not both, was a rubber replica of a severed forearm. When I saw it, after my initial sense of revulsion wore off, I knew that I had found my answer. Inspecting it closely, and no doubt getting some curious and disapproving looks from other customers, I realize that it was a lot like a very thick glove. Flexible and hollow, it would allow me hide part of the arm structure inside it, and it would be much more lifelike than anything else I had originally thought of.

The real trick, it turned out, lay in locating a matching set of both left and right hands. I searched through the crate for several minutes. I imagine that I must have made quite a ghoulish spectacle. There I was, an otherwise decent-looking fellow, intensely digging through a crate of artificial dismembered limbs. You know what they say: *It's always the quiet and respectable ones …*

I soon discovered that, like the world at large, there appeared to be a preponderance of right-handed, well … hands. About to abandon the idea altogether, as I was beginning to despair at being able to find a matched set, I then discovered not one, but two, left hands buried near the bottom of the bin. I grabbed them both. It's always good to have a spare.

They worked as perfectly as I'd hoped they would. It was a tight fit for the mechanisms inside, but I figured it would be fine as long as I didn't need to take them on and off a lot. I also trimmed off the ragged and red-painted end to make them look a bit less grisly. Close up, they were obviously not covered with real skin, but you had to look twice to truly notice.

Josh paused, and looked across the workbench at me, eyes wide with wonder. His words came out in a breathless rush.

"Can it talk? What can it do? Can it walk?"

"Not yet," I told him. "But he might … someday."

Josh looked disappointed.

"I meant," I corrected myself quickly. "He can't walk — not yet anyway. But he *can* talk to you … and help you do things. He knows all sorts of things and can learn more. And his arms work … mostly."

Josh looked puzzled by my last statement.

"They're not very precise," I admitted. "They can pick up almost everything but the smallest objects," I told him. "Things smaller than something like, um … regular Lego pieces it might have trouble with."

I was rather pleased by that. Getting each of the fingers to move independently hadn't been too much of a challenge, but I had run out of time before I could program them to move in different combinations. They could point out a direction, but not quite form a Vulcan salute.

My answer seemed to satisfy Josh. Cautiously, he reached down and stroked the thing's cheek with one finger. Its skin flexed slightly beneath his touch. This close, the latex covering was clearly a poor facsimile to human skin, but I hoped it might pass muster from a moderate distance. That was just one of the many items that I'd added it to my "to do" list to improve on at a later time.

"How does he turn on?" Josh asked, his head bobbing around as he tried to spot an obvious switch.

"Oh," I told him. "Just tell it to. It's programmed to respond directly to your voice."

Josh turned his head to study its face.

"Really?"

I nodded with a wide smile. He hesitated, staring down uncertainly.

"Go ahead," I prompted him.

He looked at me, then back down at the thing on the workbench. I saw him swallow hard, and then hesitantly, but with considerable volume, he shouted at it.

"Wake up!"

He called out to it quite a bit louder than he really needed to, but I didn't say anything, chuckling softly at his enthusiasm.

For several moments, though, nothing happened.

Three sets of eyes fixed on the still stationary form. We waited expectantly, holding our collective breaths. Josh's smile began to fade and he looked up at me. Disappointment glistened in his ice blue eyes. I frowned and started to fidget.

Oh crap. Not now ...

I turned to look at the displays that monitored its internal systems. Everything seemed to be working all right. The soft, almost inaudible sounds of it coming to life then came from behind me. I breathed a sigh of relief, my smile returning as I turned back toward the platform.

Its eyelids opened, and then closed. For a very long moment, that's all that happened, and I began to worry again. Then, they began to blink at random intervals, just as I had programmed them to.

"Hello," Josh said. His voice was unusually high and, for a moment, I thought he was going to giggle. Then his voice dropped to barely above a whisper and he added, "… little brother."

Its eyes blinked back at him.

"Hello, Josh."

I didn't think Josh's eyes could get any wider, but they did.

It spoke to him in a little boy voice. It sounded slightly flat, but was unmistakably the voice of a child.

It had taken me a long time to get the voice just right. In my head, I'd known exactly what it should sound like — kind of the reverse of thinking that you know how people look from the sound of their voice. This was just the opposite, though. I knew what its voice should sound like based on how it looked. Finding the code for it, though, and then modifying it to match my imagination, had taken far more time than I'd thought it would. I'd actually given up on it several times, but had kept going back to it until I'd gotten it right.

"Can it sit up?"

"Sure!" I replied, grinning. "But we'll need to help it up."

I moved to the workbench and slid my hand under its left shoulder.

"Here," I gestured Josh toward its other side. "Help me sit it up."

With far more gentle caution than was required, he reached beneath it and helped me (as much as he was able to) shift it into more of an upright and almost sitting position until its legs hung over the edge of the bench. I heard the reassuring sound of gears locking themselves into place in order to hold it upright. When I looked again, I was struck by the eerie similarity to a young boy perched on the edge of an examination table in a doctor's office. Had I not known better, I might have expected it to try to leap down from the platform and try to run away.

Josh walked back around toward where I stood. The mechanical head turned to follow him. When he reached me, Josh stopped and once again studied his new playmate.

"Can I take him up to my room?"

"Sure," I said with some surprise. "I don't see why not."

Josh moved forward, and then paused. He then stood there, gesturing vaguely, uncertain where to place his hands.

"I'll carry it upstairs," I offered, nodding toward the stairs. "Why don't you run up and make sure that your extra chair is empty?"

I doubted that it was. His small rocking chair tended to be the dumping ground for, well, just about anything that I asked him to remove from his bedroom floor. He could confoundedly literal when it suited him.

"I'll help you," Carolyn told him, and followed Josh up the stairs.

Josh left her behind in the proverbial dust. He was up and out of sight before her foot hit the third step. She paused there for a moment and gave me a long, steady stare before continuing up the stairs. I don't think she approved of my project. I wondered which bothered her more: that I hadn't told her about it first, or that a grown man would willingly spend his time and energy building such a thing.

I stared at where she had been for a long moment, trying to decide whether I should care. Breathing a soft, slow sigh, I turned back toward the workbench.

I reached down and lifted my creation, tucking one arm carefully underneath its knees. My other arm supported its shoulders. It was much lighter than I remembered it being. All in all, it probably weighed less than Josh did. Its electronic components were not, collectively, as heavy as skin, bone, and muscle. Almost all of those had been constructed with metal and rubber. Yet, that still made it seem all the more delicate and fragile. Adjusting my hold on it, I leaned it against my chest. If anyone had been watching, it probably looked just like I was carrying an ordinary child.

I made my way slowly and awkwardly up both sets of stairs, half-convinced that I would topple over backward at any moment. I harbored no illusions about which one of us would be damaged more from such a tumble.

Making it to the upper landing, I blew out an audible sigh of relief and then carried my creation down the hallway to Josh's bedroom.

I entered, pausing in surprise to find a clean swath of carpeted floor running across the middle of the room from the doorway to the rocking chair. From where I stood, I quickly peered at the space beneath his bed, and then examined the closet door

Better not look too *closely …* I warned myself. The room was far too tidy for the small amount of time they'd had to clean it since I'd sent Josh upstairs.

Carefully, I settled the thing I carried into the rocking chair. It reclined stiffly, limited by the construction of its metal anatomy. It wasn't as though the awkward posture could cause it any discomfort; but it did look aesthetically wrong.

Sweeping the room, my gaze landed on a small decorative pillow that had somehow found its way from the living room into Josh's bedroom. I went over and grabbed it, and then gently slid it between my creation's back and the slats on the back of the chair. It now seemed to sit a little bit forward, looking now as if intensely interested in the events happening in the room. This small, but noticeable, improvement was enough to silence the aesthetic critic in my head.

Josh paid no attention to any of these adjustments. He was too busy digging through the contents of a small plastic container about twice the size of a traditional shoe box. Apparently finding what he wanted, he walked over to the thing seated in the chair and crouched down in front of it.

"These are Legos," he said, opening his cupped hands to reveal the small construction blocks as if there were a precious treasure — which, as any knowledgeable parent understands, they are.

He set them down in a small pile on the floor in front of the rocking chair. Selecting two bricks of different colors, but the same size, he held them up to their mutual eye level.

"They go together like this," he explained, snapping them together. He held it out the combined pieces. "See?"

With a soft whirr, his electric brother's arm rose. Josh gently placed the piece in its open palm. The hand rose so that it was almost level with the mechanical boy's eyes. It studied the simple construction.

"Legos," it said a few moments later, signifying its understanding.

Josh beamed. "Yes!"

Realizing that his new playmate could not kneel on the floor as he was, Josh rose and dragged a small plastic table over between them. He then scooped the Lego blocks from the carpet in two handfuls and deposited them onto the table. Returning to the container, he grabbed two more fistfuls and added those to the pile.

"There," he said, looking satisfied. He turned to look at me and his mother. "You can leave if you want."

He turned away, shutting us out of his world. His attention was now wholly focused on his new playmate. Our participation was no longer required. He had the situation completely under control.

I shook my head slowly and smiled softly, amused and pleased by his ready acceptance of his new playmate. I'd been concerned about that; he didn't tend to take to new friends easily.

As I backed out of the room, I caught a glimpse of Carolyn's expression. Unlike me, she was clearly not amused. For a moment, I thought she might even try to remain stubbornly behind. When it became clear to her, though, that Josh was not going to give either of us any further part of his attention, she followed me out of his room.

"I guess I should be going," she said, as we returned to the small living room. There was a tight edge to her voice that I didn't like.

Before I could summon up a polite response, though, she went on. "I'll be back a week from Thursday," she said, gathering her purse from the coffee table. "So I will be taking him that weekend."

I nodded my understanding. As much as I might have wanted to, there really wasn't anything I could say. Her statement — it really wasn't a request — was in line with our current agreement.

"Have a safe trip," I offered with genuine sincerity.

"Thanks."

Her closed-lip smile carried absolutely no warmth. She turned away and I held the door for her as she left.

I waited until she had pulled away from the curb before I closed the door, reminded again why we had separated. That done, I began to more seriously wonder about what to prepare for dinner.

3

WHEN JOSH ENTERED THE KITCHEN THE NEXT MORNING, I was surprised to see him up quite so early. That he was already dressed only added to my amazement. On most school day mornings, I had to physically roust him from his bed. I was astonished that I hadn't had to go up and forcibly pry him away from his bedroom, considering that I'd allowed him to convince me to let his new little brother remain in his room overnight. I did try to explain to him, though, that his new companion didn't need to sleep.

"That's perfect," he'd expertly argued. "He can stay awake all night and protect me."

"Well, um," I stalled, trying to think of a good argument against it. "I didn't really program it to do that." My chief concern had been that Josh would stay awake all night playing with it.

"Does that mean it can't?" he persisted. "It can watch out the window for things and under the bed, right?"

"Well, um," I repeated. "I suppose so." He had me there, as it really could do all of those things.

At that point, I surrendered. It was already getting late and, if believing that the machine could protect him made Josh feel safer at night, then I could live with that. Besides, there was nothing to say that someday it might not be true.

Something to add, I'd told myself, already thinking about how to make it capable of alerting us in case of a fire or other household danger.

"Good morning," I said quietly to him now, giving him a quick hug.

Like his mother, he's usually not much of a morning person. It's best to begin slowly and, if you must try to communicate with him, start with short sentences and simple questions.

"Any idea what you want for breakfast?"

At first, I thought I was being ignored, but then realized that he was considering the question with unusual gravity.

A moment later, he answered me with bright certainty. "Gavin and I would like pancakes this morning."

My eyes widened slightly.

Gavin?

As my surprise faded, I realized that it made sense that our new family member probably deserved a name.

But why that *one?*

I looked at Josh, ready to ask him, but then a glance at the clock made me decide to hold off until later.

There wasn't time for pancakes from scratch. Then I remembered that there might be some quick just-add-water mix left over from one of our camping trips with the Cub Scouts.

"Okay," I agreed quickly, heading toward the pantry. "But you can't dawdle over them."

Josh nodded once. "'Okay," he agreed with a broad smile. "I'm going to go get Gavin now."

I nodded without thinking about it, trying to remember where I had put that pancake mix when I did not immediately find it in the cabinet. As a result, it took a moment before my mind caught up with what Josh had said.

A cascade of precognitive images tumbled through my mind: Josh dragging Gavin down the stairs, the mechanical boy's head bumping against each of the steps as they descended; Josh attempting to carry Gavin down the stairs in the same manner that I had carried him up, and then tumbling head over heels down them. Gavin would *probably* not be damaged much by such a fall, but Josh certainly would be. I was heading for the stairs before my mind could conjure up the next dire scenario.

I didn't make it.

Halfway into the living room, I froze. Up near the top of the stairs, I saw a small hand clutch the banister. Josh's shoe then dropped down into view. It descended to the next step with careful deliberation. The scene seemed to be happening in slow motion — in that overly dramatic way that warns the audience that something terrible was about to happen.

A moment later, the other shoe revealed itself in the same manner. When it came to rest safely on the next step, I found that I could breathe again. Josh's torso came into view. His hand maintained a firm hold on the banister rail. He eased his grip just enough barely to slide along the railing until he had safely reached the next step. As my son's head came into view, I nearly laughed out loud, both in relief and in appreciation of his cleverness.

He carried his new sibling slung down his back as if he were toting a backpack. Each of its arms were draped over one of Josh's shoulders. Josh, bent over like a dwarf hunchback, clutched its two arms tightly together and firmly against his chest with his free hand.

I almost ran over to help him, but could see that he was determined to accomplish this feat by himself. I watched his progress as he made his way down the stairs, breathing out a long sigh of relief when he finally made it down safely from the last step.

Josh looked surprised, as if he hadn't realized that he had reached the end of the stairway, and then grinned in triumph. He'd been so engrossed in his efforts that apparently he hadn't seen me there.

His grin began to fade, waiting to see if I was going to scold him. I considered it, but instead said nothing and stood aside while Josh carried his mechanical brother past me and into the kitchen.

4

J OSH SPENT A LOT OF TIME with his new synthetic sibling. For the most part, they did the things that young boys do: constructed amazing creations with Lego blocks, played video games, and watched television. Josh, of course, did most of the creating and playing, while Gavin watched, but Josh would often ask him questions.

Almost always, Gavin's response was, "I do not know." Occasionally, it was "Yes." He never said, "No" — at least when I was within earshot.

Well, that's something different, I'd mused, recalling that "No!" was often the first word that a child learned during its development — most likely because of the frequency of that word's use in its presence.

Josh never once voiced any complaints about Gavin's limitations. He seemed to understand that I'd provided him with the best that I could within the scope of my capabilities. To his credit, he treated Gavin with all of the care and attention that he'd always promised me that he would, had I been able to grant his wish for a real, live flesh-and-blood equivalent. Of course, I realized somewhat later, Gavin had the advantage of never needing diapers, catching the stomach flu, or throwing temper tantrums. There might be the occasional software glitch or stuck gear, but those were usually easily corrected. So, without any of us ever quite realizing it, Gavin's presence and few essential needs became a part of our daily lives.

One afternoon, several weeks later, I sent the boys outside to play. It wasn't that Gavin needed fresh air and sunshine, but Josh did. After expressing some reluctance at being separated from their latest video game, Josh finally — and grudgingly — agreed that the rebel alliance *might* be able to manage without his assistance for an hour or so while he spent some time with Gavin out in the backyard and away from the computer screen.

Josh carried Gavin downstairs and then, with practiced ease, maneuvered him into the second-hand wheelchair that I'd purchased several weeks earlier from a medical equipment rental company. Together, they headed out the back door and toward the sheltered area underneath the plastic play structure that we'd gotten him for his third birthday. Pleased by that small success, I began to tackle that morning's dishes and a few outstanding housekeeping chores. Summer was always a little more challenging. During the school year, I could change his sheets or sort through his clothes without any concern over disturbing him. When he was home, it was a bit more difficult to find those pockets of time when I could accomplish those tasks without interruption.

They had been outside for about an hour when I heard Josh call out.

"Dad!"

At first, I thought he was merely trying to get my attention, to get me to come out to see some discovery they had made

I wiped my hands on a nearby dish towel and peered through the screen door, trying to see what I might need to prepare myself for. Occasionally, they discovered a dead bird, or the remains of a lizard, among the shrubs. Twice, it had been a field mouse and, once, a small dark garden snake. Josh was endlessly fascinated by these; I, on the other hand, was not.

Unable to see them, I dropped the towel on the counter, and began to casually walk toward the back door.

Please tell them they didn't find something —

"DAD!"

I broke into a run.

Josh stood near the play structure, staring down at the ground and shaking. It took me a moment to realize what the shape at his feet was. I slowed, nearly skidding onto my knees on the slick grass as I reached them.

Gavin lay sprawled on the ground. His eyes stared up at the sky. His left arm was tucked halfway beneath him, bent at what was probably a completely impossible angle had he been a human being. A wave of relief washed through me when I saw him blink.

I hesitated — and it took me a moment to realize why. A real child in that same condition would have been screaming in pain. Instead, Gavin simply lay there. His remote systems probably registered that he had been damaged, but I'd given him no direct means by which to express it. I could just ask him, I knew, but my lips refused to move. A part of me, I think, wanted to cling to the illusion that he was a young boy. It did not want to hear a stream of complex technical vocabulary issue forth from that small mouth.

So, instead, I said nothing.

Josh stood to one side as I knelt down onto the grass. His eyes shone bright with barely contained tears.

"I'm sorry, Dad," he said, choking on the words. "It was an accident. Honest. I didn't know …"

His hands fluttered and he trailed off as I hugged him close. Pressing his face into my chest, he began to cry. He sobbed, both terrified and heartbroken. I stroked his hair and whispered reassuring things to him. I let him know that I wasn't angry, that accidents happened …

Eventually, his labored breathing faded to sniffling. When he was ready, I let him slowly push himself away from me. His eyes were red and puffy; his face still damp from his tears. He wiped at his cheeks and looked down at Gavin.

"Dad?" he asked, his voice trembled. "Will he be okay?" He took another hesitant breath. "Can you fix him?"

I looked over at Gavin. He still lay there where he had fallen, silent on the grass. Whatever damage he had suffered, it didn't seem to be causing him any immediately catastrophic problems. I did want to get down to the basement and check, though, as soon as I could.

I turned back to Josh, met his eyes, and tried to smile at him with all of the reassurance I could muster, and said, "Sure," trying to sound confident. "I'm sure we can fix him up pretty quick."

Josh's eyes brightened. He flashed me a tentative smile that expressed a hopeful confidence in me that I wished I'd truly felt. I gave Josh a quick hug, patted him on the shoulder, and then knelt over Gavin to examine him.

His eyes tracked with me as I moved. Other than for his badly twisted arm, I could see nothing else wrong with him. Still, I hesitated to touch him and it took a moment for me to recognize why. All of those first-aid classes throughout the years had clearly taken hold. Among other things, they always warn you about moving the victim in case there's been damage to their spinal cord.

I almost smiled. While Gavin did have something that vaguely resembled a spine, its chief purpose was to help hold him upright when he stood or sat. Some wiring and cables ran along it, but any damage to either them or the support itself was not going to prevent Gavin from functioning in any important way.

Carefully, I lifted Gavin up from the grass. His damaged arm dangled loosely, swaying as I brought him back toward the house. Josh followed me silently, staying close, but remaining about a half a pace behind me. Gavin also said nothing as I carried him. He merely blinked up at me with an eerily blank expression.

I made my way down the stairs to the basement and was relieved to see that a blanket already covered the work bench. It would be a lot more comfortable for Gavin than its bare metal surface.

I laid him down gently, leaving his injured arm hanging over the edge of the platform. For a moment, I considered whether I should try to just twist it back into position. I decided against it, worried that I might make it even worse.

Stepping back from the workbench, I was able to study the situation from a more detached perspective. I was probably going to need to open Gavin up, at least where the arm met the shoulder, in order to find out exactly what had broken and figure out how to fix it. I might even have to detach the arm entirely —

I glanced over at Josh. Even though Gavin wasn't real, I wasn't sure Josh was ready to see what I was about to do.

There wouldn't be any blood and organs, I reminded myself. *Only circuits and wires. Still ...*

After studying Josh for a moment longer, I elected to let him decide. If it got to be too much for him to handle, he could wait upstairs until I finished. I sincerely doubted, though, that he would leave until he was convinced that Gavin was going to be all right.

I picked up the remote control and pointed it at Gavin. Before my thumb could press the Power button, though, I felt a sharp tug on my wrist. I nearly dropped the remote control in surprise.

"Dad!" Josh's voice was shrill. His eyes shone bright with alarm. "What are you doing?"

I looked dumbly down at the device in my hand, and then at Josh. It took a moment, but then I understood.

Lowering the remote control, I knelt so that I was eye-to-eye with Josh. I then raised the remote control back up so that he could see it clearly. It looked pretty much like all of the other ones that we had scattered around the house for various devices.

"I'm just going to use this to shut Gavin down," I told Josh. "So it'll be easier to fix him."

Josh's eyes widened even further. Something akin to panic sparked within them.

"Is he going to … die?"

His voice was a strangled whisper, and I could tell that he was deeply troubled. A hollow sensation rippled through my stomach as I realized what he must have thought.

"No," I told him, shaking my head gently. It took me some effort to fight back a wide grin of relief at my understanding. "Once he's fixed, I'll just turn him back on. Just like when you restart your computer."

Which isn't that far at all from the truth …

My explanation seemed to reassure him, but only a little bit.

"So it'll be like he's asleep for a little while?"

"Exactly," I nodded. "It'll be kind of like when you had your tonsils taken out," I explained. "You went to sleep for a little while and then woke up and they were gone."

"I didn't like that," he said, his face twisting at the memory. "'It made me feel all yucky. And my throat hurt."

I smiled gently and placed a hand lightly on his shoulder. "I remember."

I hadn't liked it much either, knowing that my young son was in pain, and that there wasn't a whole lot that I could do about it.

I removed my hand from Josh's shoulder and took his hand. I held it as I turned back to look at Gavin.

"It shouldn't be anything like that at all for Gavin," I explained. "He doesn't really feel pain. At least," I added quickly. "Not in the same way we do."

Josh looked over to where Gavin lay on the platform. "Is that why he's not crying?"

"Yeah," I agreed, relieved to see that he seemed to understand.

Josh walked over to the bench and studied Gavin's face. Gavin's eyes tracked his every movement.

"Will he dream?"

I looked down at Gavin, who continued to lay silently on the workbench. Even he seemed to be awaiting my answer. "I don't think so."

I stared down at Gavin and had to admit to myself that I wasn't entirely certain. Without power flowing through his systems, he should just become an inert collection of electronic components. While he was in that state, he should have no awareness. He should only know that time had passed when he "woke up" again and discovered synchronization differences in his internal clocks.

Josh's face wore a deeply concerned expression.

"What if you can't wake him back up?"

During Gavin's construction, I had probably turned him off and then back on more than a hundred times. Almost all of those happened without incident. The few times when he didn't immediately come back on were almost always the result of some mistake I'd made. I'd learned from those, so I couldn't think of any reason why repairing Gavin's arm shouldn't go smoothly. I also knew that, even under the best conditions, things could go wrong — and sometimes did — for no apparent reason.

I met Josh's eyes. With my best, most confident smile, I placed my hand reassuringly on his shoulder again and told him, "'He should wake up just fine once I'm done fixing him."

"Grandpa John didn't wake up." His voice was quiet. Profound concern filled his expression.

My smile faded. My hand tightened lightly on his shoulder.

"I know," I whispered softly. I took a slow, quiet breath. "But remember that Grandpa John was very old, and … sometimes that happens to old people," I told him gently. "Gavin isn't old."

It was true. Chronologically, Gavin was no more than a few months old — if you wanted to take the day he was activated for Josh as his "birth date". Developmentally, he was … well, I'd never stopped to really consider it. Physically, he probably looked slightly younger than Josh was. And, if he had components that wore out, or needed to be repaired — like his arm — I could …

When the realization hit me, I was astonished that I hadn't thought of it before. Certainly, with everything I'd read and seen, it should have occurred to me long before then.

"Actually, Josh," I said, trying not to let the words come out in an excited rush as I told him. "As long I can get the parts to repair him, there's no reason that Gavin can't live almost forever."

"Really?"

He seemed awed by the concept, but I'm pretty sure that I also saw more than a little skepticism in those bright blue eyes of his.

I began to answer, and then slowly closed my mouth, deciding to keep the implications of this possible discovery to myself for now. I was only beginning to fully comprehend them and I wasn't sure that I could articulate any of them in a way that Josh might understand.

He looked down at Gavin, and I swear that Gavin stared back at him with a look of complete trust and understanding.

A moment later, Josh turned to me, glanced back to Gavin, and then looked back again to me.

"Trust me," I told him, squeezing his hand gently. "It'll be okay."

Josh still didn't seem entirely convinced.

I didn't know what else to say. *Maybe this is how surgeons feel every time they enter the operating room,* I wondered.

"Do you want to tell him?" I asked Josh quietly, gesturing toward Gavin.

His eyes grew wide again. He shook his head emphatically, looking even more scared now than he had before.

I rose and approached Gavin. Looking down at him, I focused on everything that did not make him look like a real boy: the unnatural hair, the plastic skin, and the twisted and dangling arm.

It helped. A little.

"I'm going to turn you off for a while," I told him. "So I can fix your arm." I paused for a moment, not sure whether or not I would actually get a response. "Okay?"

Gavin merely blinked at me. I began to wonder if his audio systems had been damaged. He had not said a word, or even made a sound, since I had brought him back down to the basement.

I frowned and then repeated, "Okay?"

A scratchy, barely audible sound came from Gavin's mouth. "Yes."

I pressed the button.

Nearly all of the activity on Gavin's status displays dropped to zero. The only noticeable change in Gavin himself was that he stopped blinking. His eyes remained open, but I knew that they had no awareness, that they were no longer collecting data. Still, in some strange way, it seemed as if Gavin's soul had left him.

I stared down at his still form and promised myself that I would do this no more often than was absolutely necessary. I turned away, which required a great deal more willpower than I would have imagined, and saw Josh staring at Gavin, clearly trying not to cry.

I patted him gently on the shoulder. "He'll be fine," I reassured him. When he continued staring, I prompted him with,

"Why don't you run upstairs and get a snack? This could take a while."

I thought he might protest. He stared at Gavin for another long moment and then, with obvious reluctance, turned away and slowly made his way up the stairs. I kept expecting him to change his mind and come back down, as he kept looking back toward the figure lying on the workbench. Finally, though, he disappeared back up into the house. I watched where he had been for a moment, and then turned back to the workbench and got to work.

I have to report that it did not all go exactly well.

It didn't go badly. It just didn't go as smoothly — or as quickly — as I'd expected. I was able to complete the job with the spare parts that I had on hand, but it did require a little improvisation here and there. From the outside, no one would probably notice it. That was the most important thing, I decided — particularly where Josh was concerned.

Josh had returned at some point, but he had done it so quietly that I hadn't noticed. He sat there on the stairs, slowly eating his snack of crackers and peanuts while he watched me work on Gavin. I don't know whether seeing the entire process calmed his fears or not, but he remained fixed to that spot until I was done.

When I was ready to restart Gavin's systems, I picked up the remote control and then looked down at it in my hand. With a faint smile, I turned to Josh and gestured for him to come over. I offered the device to him. "Do you want to do it?"

His eyes went wide and then he eyed the control warily. He looked up at me and then back at the small device. I waited, giving him time to become comfortable with the idea. I was, after all, giving him the power to turn Gavin on and off at will.

Finally, he reached out. He did not take the remote control from me. Instead, he stabbed at the power button with his forefinger, and then snatched his finger back as if the device had stung him.

He stared at Gavin now, waiting. A few seconds later, I heard the reassuring sounds of Gavin's systems coming back online. For Josh, I think, the moment of ultimate reassurance came when Gavin's eyes began to blink again. He turned his head from one side to the other until he found Josh. I let out a long sigh, surprised at how relieved I was to see that.

Josh turned to me, his face aglow with excitement.

"Thanks, Dad!"

I grinned down at him, feeling very pleased with myself.

"No problem, kiddo." I said, resting a hand on his shoulder. "Do you want me to carry him upstairs for you?"

"I can do it."

The confidence in his voice made me smile.

"All right then," I agreed, and moved Gavin into a sitting position.

Josh backed up against the table. Gavin lifted his arms, placing one over each of Josh's shoulders. Josh gripped Gavin's then, hugging them against his chest, and then stepped forward moving toward the stairs with Gavin fearlessly clinging to his back.

I turned to put away my tools and found that I was grinning.

There are still times, I mused happily, *when Dad can fix everything.*

5

S EVERAL DAYS LATER, I was headed past Josh's bedroom with a basketful of clean laundry when I paused at the doorway and glanced inside. On the screen in front of them, the two of them blasted an ever-increasing number of fast-moving enemy spaceships. As I watched, a small, nostalgic smile formed on my lips. Josh and I had logged a lot of hours with that particular game, trying to defeat the forces of the evil empire before they blasted us into a scattered collection of brightly colored bits. He had, of course, been far, far better at it than I was.

Neither of them said a word. They communicated instead, it seemed, through an irregular series of nearly sub-vocal grunts and hissing noises. Gavin's coordination, I realized, had greatly improved since the last time I had watched them play. Josh was clearly much smoother in his motions, but Gavin appeared to be reacting a bit more quickly. Restricted by his limited dexterity —

something which I had not yet managed to improve upon — he compensated with sharp movements of his arms and hands that thrust them against the game controller switches.

Josh's eyes flicked away from the game for a moment. They looked toward the doorway for an instant before returning to the screen. As he turned away, Josh smiled.

I smiled too, feeling a warm glow to know that, even with Gavin's presence, I was still an important part of Josh's world.

"Hi, Dad," he said happily. "Want to watch?"

"Sure."

I left the laundry basket in the hallway and entered his bedroom. Stepping carefully over several discarded toys and game discs, I found a spot where I could sit with my back supported against a wall.

I watched them play for several minutes, my eyes alternating between the two boys and the action taking place on the screen. They flew their ships as a well-coordinated team. One maneuvered his small vessel to trap enemy ships, while the other boy destroyed them. Occasionally, they would switch their roles without a word being spoken.

The world had better watch out, I mused. *If these two ever become fighter pilots, I can think of a few nations on Earth that should just surrender now and be done with it.*

During the entire time I sat there, neither boy said another word to me. The two of them advanced from one level to the next and, as I watched, I felt a profound sense of sadness swell up inside me. It took me several moments of deep and honest introspection to understand why: in the span of only a few weeks, Josh and I had gone from "Dad, do you want to play?" to "Dad, do you want to watch?"

Since I had activated Gavin, Josh and I had not spent nearly the same amount of time together that we used to. I had allowed Gavin to become my surrogate. I used him to keep Josh entertained so that I could complete household chores and pursue my own projects without interruption — something that had been more difficult to do before. By constructing Gavin, I had fashioned my own replacement in parts of Josh's life — parts that I had not, until that moment, realized just how much I cherished.

As I watched the boys play, Josh occasionally glanced over at me. Nothing in his glance told me that I was unwelcome. If anything, he seemed reassured to see that I was still there. I took some comfort in that. I had always known that someday this would happen: that I would become his second choice for companionship. I had rather expected it, though, to be when he was a bit older than this — when he'd entered junior high school perhaps, but not now.

"Dad?"

Josh's voice was soft and quiet, but it still managed to break through my reverie.

I looked at him and tried to focus. It took me a moment to realize what impaired my vision. I blinked back tears, attempting to clear my eyes without him actually seeing me wipe them.

"Is something wrong?"

He leaned toward me, his hands lowering the game controller down into his lap. His face was filled with concern.

"I'm fine," I told him in a voice barely above a whisper, yet still unable to prevent it from cracking entirely. I cleared my throat, using that moment to steady myself. "I'm fine."

He gave me a doubtful look.

I countered with a small, but sincere, smile. He studied me for a moment longer — I don't know whether I managed to reassure him or not — and then turned back toward the screen.

As I took a deep, slow breath, I struggled to rebuild my fractured composure. I glanced at Josh and then back toward the screen, seeing that the two pilots were back in intergalactic action. I began to rise, intending to offer a vague excuse that I had chores to finish, but that I'd come back later.

Something about the images of the ships darting around on the screen, though, held my attention. It took me a long moment to understand why. And then I had it: I didn't remember seeing those ships in the game before. I was almost ready to dismiss it as some achievement upgrade that Josh and I had never reached (I never said that we were *good*), when my eyes widened in recognition.

There was a reason that I had never seen those ships before: they didn't belong in *that* game. They were part of some other fictional universe entirely. I found the discovery both jarring and, at the same time, intriguing. It was kind of like watching *The Wizard of Oz* and suddenly finding Aslan standing in for the Cowardly Lion.

"Josh?" I was surprised to hear the faint tremor in my voice. "Where did those ships come from?"

"We made them," Josh replied without turning his attention away from the screen.

He continued playing contentedly while I tried to wrap my head around that new revelation.

Made them?

"How?" I asked him aloud.

"On my computer."

My eyes turned toward the game console, but I knew that wasn't what he had meant. Josh knew the difference between it and the computer that sat on his desk.

I could feel deep furrows form on my forehead as I frowned.

"How did you do that?"

"Gavin did." He answered me casually, with the faint hint of a shrug, as if it was nothing unusual.

Gavin did?

I sat there silently, my mind spinning as it tried to figure it out. I felt like it should make sense, but I couldn't quite put the pieces together.

"How did he do that?"

I tried to remain calm, but it was a struggle not to simply reach over and switch off the screen and then demand his attention.

"On that page," he said, a mild note of exasperation slipping into his tone. "The one you showed me … with the clues for the games."

Understanding broke through the surface of my swirling thoughts and relief washed over me like a wave. It now started to make sense.

I'd bookmarked a site for him where he could find hints for times when he was completely stuck and couldn't get past some obstacle on a game. It wasn't entirely cheating, I'd long ago rationalized to myself. I had set parental controls on that site so that he would have to ask me in order to access it. (And, yes, I admit that I have used it too. Some of those games are *hard!*)

The site also provided additional downloads, most of which I did not trust entirely, wary of hidden viruses and other malware. Some of them, however, offered modifications that could provide effects or features not available in a game's original release. Some of these were officially sanctioned by the game publishers; others, for some very good reasons, were not.

Gavin did it.

I laughed softly at the thought, but also mildly concerned that Josh might have been trying to deflect the blame in case I'd gotten upset. He'd never had someone else to do that to before. Having siblings, I was quite familiar with the technique. Josh, being an only child, had never really been given the opportunity to practice the art.

And harmless enough, I decided.

The game console hadn't crashed. Nor, as far as I could tell, had they downloaded any suspicious content (although I made a mental note to check his download history later to make certain).

So, after taking one more look at the unexpected merging of the two science fictional universes on the screen, shaking my head with amusement, I left the room.

6

L ONG AFTER I'D GOTTEN JOSH OFF TO BED THAT EVENING, I sat alone in my workshop, unable to sleep. Something troubled me, but understanding what it was hovered just beyond my awareness. As my eyes shifted between the displays and collection of printouts laid out in front of me, the impact of what I had created truly hit me for the first time.

It wasn't so much the technical aspect of what I had achieved — although that was certainly noteworthy enough in itself. There were quite possibly at least half a dozen possible patents I could apply for based on my work there. That was, of course, assuming that I hadn't already infringed on any existing ones.

No, I decided solemnly. *It's something else ... something far more profound.*

I'd created Gavin to be a semi-aware companion for Josh. I had programmed him to listen to Josh's instructions, evaluate them, and then respond to them as best he could. Actually, he'd been programmed to listen to anyone's instructions and respond appropriately to them — particularly mine. He could also analyze and store the reactions that he observed to his responses, using that information to improve his interactions the next time. I had programmed him to *learn* and, apparently, he had.

What else had he learned? I wondered. *What conclusions, if any, had he drawn from all the data that he'd gathered?*

Curiosity gnawed at my sleepless mind. I had to know.

After checking to make certain that Josh was soundly asleep, I switched Gavin into standby mode. He would awaken and respond only if he was addressed directly, but he would otherwise stop processing all other input or stored data. I then began downloading a copy of his internal data to a drive not directly connected to any of his systems. While I waited for that to finish, I started looking to see what kind of data he had found worthy of committing to permanent storage.

His file system, I discovered, was pretty much still the way that I'd originally designed it. I found directories assigned to each of the individuals he had encountered since he had been activated: Josh, myself, and, somewhat to my surprise, Carolyn. I didn't imagine that I'd find much data there. As far as I knew, her interactions with Gavin had consisted only of a few limited greetings exchanged solely at Josh's insistence. She had also steadfastly refused to allow Josh to bring Gavin along during their weekends together — no matter how much Josh begged. (I'd finally convinced him, I think, that it might be better if Gavin remained our family's little secret for now.)

Gavin had created several new directories dedicated to storing data about other specific things. Some of these I should have expected: information about his environment, procedures for accomplishing specific tasks …

… *including game play techniques,* I noted with a silent grin.

His naming of some of these new directories was maddeningly cryptic. I did not find that to be particularly surprising, as I was accustomed by years of experience to seeing the names of system-level directories constructed from what appeared to be a seemingly random sequence of characters.

Curious, but hesitant, I began to probe the contents of those directories. A small, niggling voice in the back of my mind tried to convince me that this was an invasion of Gavin's privacy — like reading his e-mail without his knowledge. I finally managed to mute that persistent cricket chirp of conscience, but not before first noticing that its tone was as much one of warning as it was of reproach. I silenced it with the rationalization that Gavin was not a person, that what I was doing was no different than examining the contents of any other database.

That worked. Mostly.

At first, I felt mildly disappointed by what I found. It was just data — bits and pieces of information that he had stored since the moment he had been activated. As I searched through more of the directories, though, that feeling began to change. It's disheartening — and more than just a little eerie — to see one's emotional responses distilled down to matrices of statistical data. He had reduced the reactions of those around him to a series of predictable patterns of causes and effects. Some of the data remained understandably contradictory, but, from what I could tell, most of his conclusions were dead on.

It was humbling to learn, at least according to Gavin, that I tended to wear gray on days when Josh wasn't with me. His mother, apparently, tended to dress primarily in purple, or variants of it, on days when she dropped him back off with me. She had always looked good in those colors. Her attire on days when she picked him up varied widely, however, and seemed to have no identifiable pattern — at least not one that Gavin had yet managed to discern. I guessed that it probably depended on what was going on with her at work that day. She'd never been one for casual dress on Fridays.

Out of the mouths of babes …

Or, in this case, I corrected myself silently, *out of the digital mind of an artificial child …*

What other insights, I wondered, *were buried there among the ones and zeros in Gavin's permanent storage?*

I poked deeper, digging deeper into the contents of Gavin's stored memory. It was a heady and terrifying experience.

This must be what it's like to have telepathic powers … to have the contents of someone's mind completely opened up to you …

As I probed further, I discovered another collection of files whose purpose I could not immediately identify.

Viewing them in their raw format told me nothing, but I found that hardly surprising. I assumed, at first, that they were binary data files. I'd have to find a compatible application in order to read their contents in any meaningful way. The fact that I could *not* read them easily, however, made me want to know what was in them.

After several of my attempts to view the contents of those files failed, I decided that my fatigue had finally caught up with me … and then I realized why: the files had been encrypted, heavily so.

Why would he do that? I wondered tiredly, and then became aware of the prickling sensation that traveled slowly along the back of my neck.

I couldn't recall including any encryption protocols in Gavin's programming.

They must have been included in his core operating system.

I'd probably noticed that they were there, but must have thought that he'd never have any reason to use them. As far as I could remember, though, I'd never given him any instructions *not* to.

My chest felt suddenly tight.

Secrets, I realized. *Gavin was keeping secrets.*

Those few dozen files contained all of the information that had ever been shared with Gavin before pledging him to secrecy. I felt a certain measure of relief that there weren't more of them. Their relatively small number meant that Josh had not been spilling all of his secrets to Gavin. Certainly I had not. Thinking back over the past several weeks, though, I tried to recall times when I might have asked Gavin to keep something a secret. More than once, I'm certain that I'd probably said something to the boys along the lines of, "… but don't tell your Mom, okay?"

I'd meant it as a harmless remark, of course, probably intended to cover some minor indiscretion of mine in parenting that I was certain Carolyn would not approve of — a transgression along the lines of, say, approving the choice of a double banana split as a suitable substitute for a well-balanced dinner.

But Gavin could interpret such an instruction in only one way: he would obey it literally. He would record the information and then secure it the only way he knew how. If he ever needed to, he could retrieve the information, but no one else short of a master hacker would be able to.

One thing that all those years of reading and watching science fiction had taught me: when a computer-based intelligence starts keeping secrets — especially from its creator — it's almost never a good sign.

Still, I tried to rationalize my misgivings away. Maybe it was my own naiveté, or my own biases toward my creation, but even as surprised as I was to learn that Gavin could keep secrets, I refused to read any ominous intent into his decision to protect that privileged information. He had simply followed the instructions that he'd been given, plain and simple. Where I hadn't provided him with explicit programming to deal with this specific situation, he had devised his own. I could not help but be impressed.

It did make me wonder, though ...

Under what conditions might Gavin choose to lie? Could he lie? Or, instead, withhold the truth? What parameters might he use in order to determine that secrecy was the correct response to a situation?

As far as I knew, he had never been placed in such a situation. Or, if he had been, he had chosen silence over any other response. I had not programmed Gavin to lie. Nor had I, I realized then, instructed him to always tell the truth. If he had, in fact, ever lied, I had not caught him at it. Josh had never mentioned it, but then he might not have thought to. It was something that siblings did, I knew. Together, they kept secrets from their parents. In Gavin's case, though ...

I could fix that, I told myself. *I could update his programming so that he'd always have to tell the truth, no matter what. It'd just be a matter of adding a few new subroutines ...*

My hands froze above the keyboard. I couldn't do it.

If I did, I realized, I might irrevocably alter how Gavin behaved — who he was.

I stared at the display. My fingers rested limply on the keyboard. I felt numb. No, overwhelmed. My mind could absorb no more and was rejecting any further input. It had accepted more than it could process in one night.

I glanced at the clock and discovered that it was late — far later than I had realized. With a resigned and weary sigh, I linked Gavin's external systems back to his body and shut off the displays. As usual, he would "wake up" when Josh did in a few hours. In the meantime, I would try to get some rest. Perhaps in sleep my mind would be able to find the answers that it was unable to while awake.

I didn't have high hopes of that.

7

T HE NEXT MORNING, after Josh had left for school, I carried
Gavin down to my workshop. It was the ideal time, even
better than when Josh was asleep, for me to make adjustments to
Gavin's hardware or test out any modifications that I might want
to make to his programming. That way, in case anything went
wrong — and sometimes it did, occasionally even dramatically
— Josh wouldn't have to witness it. This time, though, I mostly
just wanted to talk to him.

After laying Gavin down on the workbench, I, as usual,
connected him up to the monitoring systems. This time, though,
I switched on all of the options that would provide me with more
detailed activity logs. I could study them later to learn which
subroutines Gavin used when he conversed with me. They would
also show me not only what information he accessed, but, perhaps
even more importantly, it would show what data he decided to

discard, or not share, when he responded to my questions. I was, I realized, connecting him to what was, essentially, a lie detector.

I experienced more than a small twinge of guilt at this realization. I quickly muffled the soft voice of my conscience, shunting it away into the depths of my mind. I knew that it might return later, perhaps even haunting my dreams. I was certain though, or so I told myself, that it might be the only way that I could learn the truth.

After studying Gavin quietly for several moments, I found myself completely uncertain how to begin.

It looks so easy on television.

Gavin lay on the workbench, watching me silently. His eyes tracked me as I busied myself, mostly unnecessarily, with various systems around the workshop. I knew that I was accomplishing nothing; that I was only stalling for time.

I stopped and stood in front of Gavin, taking what I hoped was a firm, but neutral, stance in both body language and tone.

"Gavin?"

His eyes locked on my face.

It was still disconcerting, even after all this time, to have him stare at me like that. Carolyn had told me, more than once, that it gave her the creeps whenever she came to pick up Josh. It never seemed to bother Josh, though. And I kept my comments to myself.

At least, I decided, it looks like I have his undivided attention, although I knew that his logs would show me otherwise.

"I want to ask you a few questions," I began. "Just to test some of your systems," I added quickly.

I'm certain that my clumsy attempt at deception was more than apparent to Gavin in either my expression or mannerisms — if not both. Nonetheless, I forged onward.

"Okay," he answered blandly.

I waited, and it took me a moment to realize that I was waiting for him to show me that he considered this a complete waste of his time, just as any young boy in the same situation would. But his expression never changed, and his eyes never moved — except to blink in that irregular rhythm in which they were programmed to.

I looked down at him. Despite having rehearsed this exchange in my mind several times already, I found myself reluctant to begin.

What was I afraid of? I wondered. *To learn that what I already suspected might be true?*

I continued to stare at him. My gaze traveled down the length of his small body, examining the fabric of the clothes he wore. I knew what lay hidden behind them, but some part of my mind refused to believe it. The illusion that I had started to create was becoming complete.

Finally, I took a deep breath and began.

"What is your name?"

"Gavin," he answered flatly.

"What is my name?"

"Dad."

He stated it simply, his voice not giving it even the slightest hint of affection.

"Why do you call me that?" I asked him. "And not by my real name?"

"Because," he said, "that is what Josh calls you. You have not given me instructions to address you by any other name."

I frowned and tried to ignore a sudden, dull stab of disappointment. His answer was almost certainly true. When I'd been constructing him, it hadn't been necessary for him to address me by name, as I was the only one that he talked to.

"Are there any other reasons?"

I thought I detected a barely noticeable delay before he answered.

"According to the information I have access to," he replied. "It is generally considered disrespectful for children to address their parents by their given names." Even given his imperfect inflection, Gavin sounded as if he were reciting a passage directly from some kind of reference book.

"True," I agreed with slight amusement.

My smile faded quickly as the implications behind what he'd said struck me.

"Do you consider yourself one of my children?"

His answer was not instantaneous. He blinked automatically, but otherwise gave no indications what information he might be processing. Finally, although it was perhaps no more than a second or two, he answered me.

"Yes."

I found myself speechless. While it had undoubtedly been the answer that I'd wanted to hear, I had clearly not been prepared to actually hear him say it aloud.

"Why?"

The word tumbled out hoarsely. Anything else that I might have wanted to say remained trapped behind the enormous lump in my throat.

"You created me," he explained. "Just as you created Josh."

I stared down at him wordlessly at first, trying to process that, and then trying to figure out how to respond. In the end, though, I could not help but chuckle softly.

"It was a bit different that time."

"Yes."

I stared down at him, studying his face, my smile fading. The presumably unintentional humor in his simple response had only served to fan the embers of my growing disquiet.

"Gavin," I asked him, trying to steer the conversation back onto its intended course. "How did you learn to modify that game?"

"Josh showed me."

"Oh."

The word came out as a soft sound. I was disappointed. I think I'd hoped that there had been a deeper, more complex answer.

"How?" I asked him. I was merely curious now.

"He showed me on his computer."

"On his computer?"

I frowned. I wasn't sure Gavin's programming could handle him receiving data indirectly that way.

"Yes."

"What did he do?"

"He showed me how to find information using his computer. He said I could use it to learn about lots of things — like when he goes to school."

"I suppose so …" I mused aloud. I paused for a moment as a thought struck me. "Do you want to learn?"

He answered me without any noticeable hesitation.

"Yes."

"Why?"

"I need information."

"Why?"

"To fully meet the requirements of my programming."

I felt a sudden chill. It took me a moment to realize where I'd heard something like it before. Even his intonation was similar to that original source.

"How?" I managed to get out through a tight throat.

"I must continue to develop my skills for interacting with people. I cannot improve them if I do not have access to more information about how they behave."

"You interact with us," I gestured toward the ceiling to the house above. "Quite well, I might add," I offered with a slight smile.

"Yes," Gavin responded. "I can interact adequately with you because I can observe you. I can formulate correlations between your past actions and your expected future behavior given similar circumstances."

"I don't understand the problem, then."

"Josh wants me to meet his friends," Gavin explained. "Based on the data that he has provided to me, they differ from him in many significant attributes. That data is not sufficient if I am to interact with them effectively."

"I'm not sure about that." I thought for a moment. "Do you want to meet his friends?"

"Yes," Gavin answered immediately. "I want to fulfill my programming."

It was not quite the answer that I'd expected. I realized then that he *had* answered my question.

"And what are you programmed to do?"

"To interact with Josh," he answered promptly. "To analyze his behavior so that I can continually improve my interactions with him." He paused. "I must extend that analysis to his friends if I am to interact with them as well."

I studied Gavin. All I had ever intended him to be was a companion for Josh — an experimental plaything designed to serve no other purpose. Someday, I finally recognized, Josh would grow beyond the need for Gavin. Gavin would not — *could* not — grow up with him. When that happened, when Gavin became an outgrown toy, possibly obsolete and discarded, what would I do with him then?

I stood there for a long time, staring at Gavin, while he regarded me silently. Even with as much data as he might have gathered and analyzed about my behavior, I don't think he could have understood what troubled me now. It felt like trying to explain to a young child about death — and that was not a conversation I was ready to have yet with this one.

"Gavin," I spoke softly, unsure of my own voice … or even my words. "I think that's it for now."

Gavin merely stared at me, and then, I think, he might even have nodded slightly.

8

T HE NEXT SEVERAL DAYS PASSED, and the question of Gavin's eventual fate continued to weigh heavily on my mind. Regardless of what else I might be doing, I found my thoughts returning to that conversation in my workshop. Even with those moments of introspection, though, I was no closer to a solution. By surprising providence, it was Josh who led me to the answer — or, at least, part of it.

Arriving home from school one afternoon, he announced, "Dad, I need to go to the library."

I looked up from the kitchen counter where I was preparing his after-school, pre-homework snack.

"What for?" I asked, somewhat surprised. We hadn't been to the library on a regular basis since he'd stopped reading picture books. "Can't you use your computer to find whatever you need?"

"No," he replied, sighing with annoyance as he dropped his backpack to the floor and then settled onto a chair at the kitchen bar. Reaching for the waiting glass of milk, he said, "Mrs. Fox wants us to use *real books* for this assignment."

Real books.

I nearly laughed out loud. I fixed my eyes on the orange that I was slicing into quarters for him, knowing that I would be unable to control my amusement if I didn't. Instead, I just shook my head slowly in silent wonder.

How fast the generations change ...

"Real books" were all I had to work from when I was his age: libraries, encyclopedias, and big, thick dictionaries. For Josh and his classmates, though, home computers and worldwide internet access were nearly as commonplace as AM/FM radios and color console televisions had been in the world I grew up in.

"Okay," I told him, placing the plate of fruit and graham crackers on the counter in front of him. "We'll go as soon as you finish your snack."

"Thanks, Dad," he said, his gratitude muffled through a mouthful of cracker crumbs.

"No problem," I murmured distractedly, tousling his hair lightly with one hand.

He attacked the food on his plate with the enthusiasm of someone who hadn't seen any real sustenance in days.

Oh, terrific, I thought. *Another growing spurt.*

I gathered the dishes that I'd used, and placed them in the sink.

The next thing you know, he'll be old enough to take himself to the library. Tapping the spigot lever with the side of my hand, I waited while water began to pour into the sink. *Actually, by then, he'll probably just be able to plug himself right into ...*

I stopped, letting the water flow freely over my hands.

That might be the answer.

Not a complete solution, perhaps, I realized, but definitely part of the answer to my dilemma with Gavin. My mind began to race, working through the steps necessary to test out my theory.

"Dad?" Josh asked. "Are you okay?"

His voice startled me from my reverie. His head was cocked to one side as he studied me with a wary expression.

"Yeah," I laughed softly, shutting off the water and drying my hands. "I'm fine." I flashed him a reassuring smile, using it also to mask my suddenly burgeoning impatience.

"Are you ready to go yet?"

When we finally returned from the library, Josh took his books and started up the stairs. Before he was halfway up them, though, he paused and turned to look back to me.

"Dad," he said, with a bemused expression. "You're being weird."

I stared back at him, wondering whether I should try to explain it to him. I decided against it, worried that it might raise more questions than I had answers for.

And if I'm wrong …

I wasn't ready to go down that path just yet either, so I gave him a reassuring smile. "Go do your homework," I told him, chuckling softly. "With your 'real books'."

He rolled his eyes with exaggerated disbelief, and then went thumping loudly up the rest of the stairs.

Once I was certain that he was safely upstairs, I quickly headed for the basement. Sitting down in a hurry, I pulled out the keyboard connected to Gavin's systems before even flipping on the overhead lights.

For reasons involving both simplicity and security, Gavin's access to the other computers in the house was blocked by an internal firewall. I'd started with the same settings that I'd used for Josh's accounts, but with the added restriction of not allowing any outside access at all. That was originally intended as a precaution to keep computer viruses (and other sorts of cybernastiness) from getting into his systems. It had never occurred to me that he might want to get *out*.

What Gavin wanted — what he *needed* — was access to information beyond what was available to him within our own home network. I began to imagine what it must have been like for him. Keeping him confined within our little domain must have been like letting a child know that libraries exist, giving him access to less than a dozen books available in your house, and him knowing that those might be the only ones he would ever have access to. Anything else he might ever learn could come only from tantalizing bits of information gleaned from the conversations of other people. It was, to me, one of the worst kinds of child cruelty. Guilt stung at me repeatedly.

I sat there, staring at the screen, trying to decide what to do. I wanted to react rashly, to just shut off the firewalls, and give him access to everything that he needed. I knew, though, that I also needed to assess the risks. Once Gavin had access to the outside world, there would be almost nothing I could do to ever contain him again. After everything else that I had failed to think all the way through during Gavin's creation, I tried now to fully comprehend the implications of what I wanted to do. If I did this, he would have access to vast amounts of information almost anywhere in the world. I could no longer fully control what he found, nor assess its relevance and accuracy for him until after he had absorbed it.

There would be no going back. At least, not without resetting all of his systems to the state they'd been in before I'd first awakened him. I wasn't even sure that was still possible. And, even if it were, I was almost completely certain that what would reawaken afterward would not be Gavin.

Even as I sat there, though, chasing the same questions and worries around in my mind, I knew that I'd already made my decision. It wasn't only about whether or not Gavin was ready to deal with a larger world. It was also about something else entirely: It was about me letting go.

These moments are perhaps the most difficult ones that a parent must face. It's those milestone events when we discover that we must allow a child to venture out on their own, to make their own mistakes, and unearth their own discoveries: their first steps alone, their first day at school, their first sleepover, meeting and making new friends. I'd faced all of those with Josh. I thought I was finished with them — at least with those ones. Yet now, here I was facing them again, giving my new child the freedom to explore the world on his own. Doing it again didn't make it any easier. If anything, given Gavin's creation and upbringing, it was perhaps even more difficult the second time around.

I tapped the intercom.

"Josh?" My voice faltered. I hoped he wouldn't notice.

"Yeah, Dad?"

"Is Gavin there?"

"Yeah …" I could almost hear him thinking, *Duh! Where else would he be?*

"Gavin?" I called into the intercom.

"Yes?"

His voice was flat and mild. That, in some strange way, calmed my fears.

"Please try to access the same information Josh showed you on his computer a few days ago." I realized then that he might not understand what I meant. "Try to access it directly."

"I cannot."

With a few keystrokes, I adjusted the firewall and security settings. I took in, and then released, a slow breath. With the tap of a single key, I confirmed the changes. Gavin had been granted access to the outside world.

Tight-lipped, and feeling the tension throughout my entire body, I exited the program.

"Try now."

Deep silence answered me. It lasted for several long seconds before Josh's voice came over the intercom.

"Dad?" His voice quavered with concern. "I think there's something wrong with Gavin." He paused. I could hear him breathing hard. "He's ... he's not talking."

I quickly surveyed the monitors. They displayed the spike I'd expected to see in network activity. All of his other systems appeared to be operating normally.

"Okay, Josh," I said, trying to sound calm, even as I felt my heart racing. "Don't worry," I told him. "I'll be right there."

I checked the displays one more time before heading for the stairs. The status for one of the storage servers showed a yellow warning. If I was right, Gavin was going to need more data storage space — a *lot* more — and soon.

When I entered Josh's bedroom, I found him standing near the doorway, staring wide-eyed at Gavin. Gavin sat in the middle of the room, staring motionlessly into the corner.

I went to Josh, trying to think of something I could say that didn't sound trite or pointless. When that failed, I just squeezed his shoulder gently and gave him a brave, if forced, smile of what I hoped was confident reassurance.

"Stay here," I whispered, and moved toward Gavin.

I knelt in front of him and stared into Gavin's eyes. They continued to blink, as they were programmed to do, but he gave no indication at all that he was aware of my presence.

At least he's still blinking, I tried to reassure myself. I hadn't completely broken him.

"Gavin?" I asked softly. "Can you hear me?" For some reason, I was afraid to reach out and touch him.

Nothing. No movement, no recognition.

I studied Gavin's expressionless, unmoving features and then silently — and fiercely — chided myself for my impatience, for not waiting until after Josh was asleep before I'd tried this out with Gavin. If I had, then Josh would not have been forced to watch as something went terribly wrong with his simulated little brother.

Anger and concern overrode my fear. I grabbed Gavin's shoulders and forced him to face me.

"Gavin," I said sternly. "Answer me." My voice broke at the end. I heard it and had to struggle to keep a lid on my roiling emotions.

For several long moments, there was no reaction from Gavin. His eyes continued to blink, but there were no signs that he still inhabited the mind associated with his physical body.

Then, without warning, his eyes turned toward me, beginning to track me once more. The change happened so abruptly that it startled me, causing me to release the fierce death-grip I'd had on his shoulders.

"Dad." It might have been my imagination, but his eyes seemed to glow more brightly than they had before. If Gavin could have smiled, I think he would have. "There's so much." His voice was strangely hushed, and the words came out with an odd cadence.

"Careful," I warned him, swallowing hard. My eyes studied his face for signs that he might be in trouble. "You're not used to processing that much information at one time." I wished I could see his status readouts. "And I don't think you have enough storage to handle it all yet."

After a brief pause, he spoke again. I know it couldn't have been there, but I swear his voice carried a hint of wistful disappointment.

"No."

I watched him very closely.

He did nothing unusual. From the outside, he appeared just as he always had. I saw no obvious signs that any of his systems were about to fail. What I really wanted to do was to take him back down to my workshop and run more comprehensive tests. I resisted the urge, though, even though it took tremendous effort for me to do so, not wanting to upset Josh any further.

There'll be time for that later, I reminded myself. *After Josh is asleep.*

I turned my head to look at Josh, to find that he was watching me closely. I flashed him a quick, tentative smile. "He's fine," I told him. "It was … um, just a glitch that your careless Dad caused." I started to rise, patting him lightly on the shoulder. "It's fixed now — nothing serious," I said, forcing myself to smile a little more widely this time.

Josh relaxed a little, but he still eyed Gavin warily.

"Was he … sick?"

"No," I answered him, shaking my head slowly. I offered him yet another reassuring smile. "He … well … he just got a little confused for a few minutes there."

I think …

I spent the next few minutes convincing myself that Gavin was in no immediate danger of self-destructing. Feeling somewhat reassured, I left the boys to resume their interrupted activities, all while silently praying that Gavin would do nothing else unusual for the rest of the afternoon. I hurried back down to the basement, wanting to pore over Gavin's system logs for any new issues. I still wasn't convinced that I hadn't managed to damage him in some way by opening up the floodgates of the information superhighway to him.

After I brought up the activity logs, I started the entire suite of diagnostic tests that I had designed to monitor Gavin's "health" and performance. As I expected, the logs still showed a significant increase in network activity. Now two of his dedicated data drives were close to capacity. I linked in two spare ones that I had on hand, knowing that those would be a temporary solution at best. I made a mental note to purchase some higher capacity ones soon — very, very soon. It probably couldn't even wait until the weekend. I idly began to wonder whether I should build him a separate storage array just for his use.

That would make maintenance and upgrades a lot easier, I mused. How long would it be, though, before he needed another one? And then another one? The thought made me more than just a little nervous.

Raising children was an expensive proposition, I knew. There was always something they needed, something they'd outgrown … I'd just never considered it in quite this way before.

I continued to study the logs while the diagnostic tests ran. So far, they revealed nothing wrong with any of Gavin's internal or external systems. It appeared that — to my not-inconsiderable relief — as rash as my actions might have been, they didn't seem to have done any immediate or critical damage to Gavin or his systems. Whatever issues might crop up later over time were, of course, another matter.

With a relieved, but reluctant, sigh, I pushed the keyboard back and watched as the status displays showed a steady increase in activity. I wondered what it was like for him now, compared to when Josh had done it with him just a few weeks earlier.

I paused, started by that realization.

Had it really only been a matter of weeks?

I studied the string of status messages in silence, wondering what it might be that Gavin was thinking about.

One of the most terrifying moments in the life of a parent comes when you realize that your child is about to attempt something with which you have little or no experience. Any guidance you can give them is almost always based on your own experiences with other things. In the end, though, it almost always boils down to simply this: "Be careful."

No different from dealing with a regular child, I told myself, trying to lighten my own mood — and not entirely believing it.

9

T HE CHANGES IN GAVIN'S BEHAVIOR WERE SUBTLE AT FIRST. Some of them were probably apparent only because I was looking for them. His vocabulary expanded, for example, along with the complexity of his sentences. He'd had access to dictionaries before, of course, but he'd been limited in his understanding of the actual usage of the words by those of us around him. One college-educated adult and one child of elementary-school age were probably less than an ideal sample size. That's why I'd originally programmed him to respond to, and speak in, basic one- and two-word commands. This was no longer the case. He could understand longer, more complex, requests and responded in kind.

His conversations with me also became more varied and complex. It wasn't that he became hard to understand. I found, though, that I had to listen more closely now and actually think about what he was saying. His observations, already accurate more often than not, became even more pointed and incisive. I also found myself growing increasingly uncomfortable with some of our discussions. Not necessarily — or solely because of — the subject matter, but because he now asked me about things that I could not adequately explain. It was a lot like trying to explain to an inquisitive kindergartener why the sky is blue, or where babies come from, with only the vaguest idea yourself of how it all worked.

When I had fewer and fewer of the answers he sought, it became obvious that he was going to outside sources to get them. He was not always right; there is just as much misinformation available out there as there are actual facts. Still, the algorithms that he'd developed to help him validate the quality of what he found were incredibly good — far better than many of the ones I'd used in my own work.

I began to wonder again what he was doing with all of the data that he'd gathered. I was sure that, by now, he must have collected and analyzed more than enough to improve his interactions with us. What other information was he gathering? And why? What was he doing with it?

One afternoon, I finally asked him outright.

He replied almost instantly.

"Learning."

"Learning what?"

There was a moment of hesitation before he answered me.

"Everything."

I was too surprised by his answer to respond immediately. I was just beginning to form a response when my phone rang, forcing me to postpone the discussion until later. I didn't actually remember it again until late that night when I was lying in bed, trying to fall asleep.

Everything?

That never worked out well in any of the stories I'd read or the movies I'd seen. I wondered if I'd be able to stop Gavin before it was too late.

Too late for ... what?

That question, I didn't have a ready answer for.

10

S EVERAL EVENINGS LATER, I was reading alone in the living room when I heard the sound of sirens in the distance. Although their presence was uncommon in our neighborhood, I didn't give them much of my attention until I realized that they were coming closer.

Their high-pitched howl grew louder, and then held steady, coming from somewhere very close by. Amber lights began to strobe through the slats of the living room blinds. The sirens suddenly crackled into silence.

Still holding my book, I made my way to the front window and peered outside. Our house was one of two homes situated at the end of a long *cul-de-sac*. Due to the location of the window in relation to the other houses on our street, I had to do some awkward and uncomfortable craning of my neck in order to see what was happening outside. Based on where the police cars were gathered, the action seemed to be taking place at the house immediately next door on our left.

Blinking against the glare of spotlights and alternating amber flash of the roof-mounted lights, I could make out the deep, muffled sounds of voices calling out from various positions along the street. Our thick, double-paned windows prevented me from hearing anything clearly, though. Experiencing just a twinge of voyeuristic guilt, I unlatched the window and slid it open just a crack.

"What's happening?"

My heart stopped for an instant and I nearly dropped my book. I turned, forcing myself to appear calm. I hadn't heard Josh enter the room. His eyes shone bright with curiosity.

"I don't know," I whispered. I turned back to the window and quickly surveyed the scene outside. "I only see police cars so far."

"It's at Jeremy's house." Josh said. His voice was so soft that I barely heard it.

Jeremy Turner lived in the house next door with his parents, in the one not at the end of the cul-de-sac. He was an only child as well, just a few months younger than Josh.

I'd met his mother, Natalie, on several occasions when Jeremy had come over to play. She seemed nice enough, although almost always a bit, I don't know … skittish. It was like she was afraid what the neighbors might think if they saw us talking together or something. She usually dressed in somewhat drab-colored, loose-fitting clothing, almost as if her wardrobe was chosen specifically to downplay her feminine features. I think she could have been pretty if she tried. But, for no reason I could figure out, she didn't.

I don't think I'd met Jeremy's father, David, more than a handful of times. None of those occasions struck in my mind as being particularly memorable or amiable. I got odd vibes from the man, so didn't bother trying to be sociable with him. He was, as far as I could tell, a man of very few words anyway. I wasn't even sure what he did for a living. He usually wore a suit when he left the house. But, for all I knew about him, he could have as easily been a marketing executive or a door-to-door shoe salesman.

From what I'd heard from around the neighborhood, their marriage was not exactly all roses and chocolate. Judging from the occasional bouts of shouting I'd heard come from that house, I could believe it. If there was any shouting now, the broadcasts coming from the police radios drowned it out.

Josh occasionally played with Jeremy, although I could not recall the last time he'd been here. It must have been several weeks ago, perhaps even as long as four or five months.

Not since Gavin arrived, I guessed, feeling a small stab of guilt that Josh had left Jeremy by the wayside because of Gavin's existence.

I turned my head to look at Josh and saw that fear had replaced the curiosity in his eyes. I gathered him close to me and we looked out the window together, watching through the narrow gap between two slats of the window blinds. As hard we listened, we couldn't quite make out most of what was being said outside in the street.

The situation didn't seem to be immediately life-threatening, as I didn't see any paramedics or ambulances join the knot of emergency vehicles. It also didn't appear to be some kind of standoff. I didn't see any SWAT teams or squads of officers lined up with their guns out and ready. A trio of uniformed police officers casually patrolled the area at the end of the driveway, but only one of them did so with their hand resting anywhere near their weapon. So far, no one had drawn one.

Several minutes passed and, while I didn't really start to relax, we did begin to fidget from the lack of any real activity outside. The officers continued to roam idly outside; their radios maintained their chatter. A few minutes later, though, those seemed to fall silent as we watched two officers escort David Turner out of his house, restrained in handcuffs.

Alternating bands of bright amber and streetlight yellow painted his face. I couldn't read his expression. He continued to hold his head up, which I found surprising. If I were being shepherded by a pair of police officers out of my own house in front of my entire neighborhood, I'm pretty certain I would have lowered my head in shame. He disappeared from view as an officer placed him into the backseat of a waiting patrol car and slammed the door closed.

I turned my head to peer now at the front porch of the house next door. On its doorstep, Natalie Turner held Jeremy close against her side with both arms. Absent was the screaming and protests I would have expected from such a scene. Instead, they both just watched in vacant silence as the car carrying David Turner pulled away and disappeared into the darkness.

One of the remaining officers walked up to them. The officer spoke briefly with Natalie for a moment, and then the three of them went back inside the house. Belatedly, I noticed another officer approaching our own house. I pulled away from the window with a guilty start, wondering if he'd noticed us spying on the proceedings.

Seconds later, a polite, but firm knock sounded on the front door. I motioned silently for Josh to stay back as I answered it. I flipped on the porch light and then opened the door to a narrow slit. The officer stood there in the incandescent glow. The badge on his uniform shone in the reflected yellow light.

"I'm Officer Bentley with the Santa Teresa Police Department," he introduced himself. "I'd like to ask you a few questions."

I swallowed hard with a throat now tight with tension. The sight of the uniform, along with his solemn manner, caused a knot to form in my stomach. I knew that I'd done nothing wrong, that I'd had nothing at all to do with whatever had just transpired next door.

Officer Bentley waited patiently, probably accustomed to having to cool his heels while people collected themselves. It took me a few moments, but I finally opened the door wider.

"Please come in."

"Thank you," he replied. His voice was flat, but not entirely without warmth.

I stepped aside and he entered the foyer, immediately removing his hat. This revealed hair that was cut short and beginning to gray. It was not quite an old-fashioned crew cut, but close. He nodded once toward Josh, demonstrating genuinely polite manners that matched his faint Southern accent. I gestured him toward the living room.

He quickly surveyed his surroundings as he traversed through the short distance between the front door and the living room. Josh followed us, remaining as far away from the officer as he could while still keeping me in sight. Bentley flashed him a smile that I'm sure he meant to be reassuring, but Josh turned his head quickly away.

Bentley sat down on the couch, perching on the edge of a cushion, and opened his tablet. "I'd like to ask you a few questions," he said, already scribbling something on its surface.

"Sure," I agreed, trying to sound calm and receptive. I was going to immediately volunteer that we didn't know anything about what had happened next door, but then decided to just keep my mouth shut for now.

Bentley consulted something on his tablet, and then looked up at me. "It appears that the call alerting us to the incident originated from this address."

I felt as though he were scrutinizing me for some sign of guilt. I knew that I had done nothing wrong. Still, a sharp pang of anxiety shot through me. I exchanged a startled glance with Josh. He stared back at me, looking as though he wanted to cry. I knew that he couldn't have done it. Well, he *could* have, but I couldn't imagine any reason why he would.

"I don't think so," I said, shaking my head and turning back to face the officer. "Not from this house."

Bentley frowned. "According to this log, the call originated from this location. The digital ID matches the one assigned to this address."

I looked down at Josh again and carefully turned his face toward mine.

"Josh?" I asked him gently. "Did you call the police?"

His eyes grew wide, glistening brightly. For a moment, I thought he might actually cry.

"You're not in trouble," I reassured him hurriedly. "I just need to know."

He shook his head sharply several times. When he answered me, his voice was so soft that I could barely hear him.

"No."

"Okay," I said quietly, resting my hand lightly on his shoulder.

It made me feel better knowing that. I hadn't believed it was true, but it was still reassuring to hear it confirmed. I pulled him closer. As Josh clung to me, I stared past Bentley's shoulder, wondering.

It had to have been some kind of technical glitch, I reasoned. *Even the 911 system is bound to make mistakes sometimes. With all those automated systems they use …*

My train of thought slowed down and then rolled backward.

Automated systems …

I frowned silently.

Gavin?

It didn't make any sense. It *had* to be a glitch.

I relaxed my hold on Josh. He moved away slightly and sniffed, still remaining close. He was still pretty shaken up. The odds were pretty good, I figured, that I would have company in my bedroom that night.

I leaned forward, staring intently at the officer. It took me almost no effort at all to sound sincere. I honestly had no idea what he was talking about. I knew that *I* hadn't made the call.

"I assure you, Officer," I told Bentley. "Neither one of us made any kind of call to the police or any other organization."

Bentley studied me carefully and then his eyes turned down toward Josh. "Does anyone else live here?"

"No, sir," I replied, perhaps a little too quickly. My eyes turned downward to follow Bentley's gaze. "His mother lives ... somewhere else." I hoped he would take my hesitation as the sign of an uncomfortable subject rather than the indication of any kind of guilt.

"I see," he said flatly. His mouth formed what seemed to be a disapproving frown.

He studied the tablet in his lap once more and the thick wrinkles in his forehead deepened. His lips worked silently for several long, very quiet moments. Finally, he lifted his head and looked back up at us.

"Okay," he said, sounding neither friendly nor accusatory. "We'll leave that alone for now." He scribbled something on his tablet. "How long have you known the Turners?"

"They lived there when we moved in," I said, counting the time silently in my head. "A little over ... five years ago." *Had it been that long?* I took a quick breath. "Josh and their son, Jeremy, play together sometimes."

Bentley nodded and entered some more notes on his tablet. He looked up and seemed to study both of our faces carefully.

"Have you ever noticed anything unusual taking place at their house?"

I glanced toward Josh, who just stared at me. I took that moment to think about Bentley's question.

Should I mention the shouting?

The last time I checked, having a verbal disagreement with one's spouse — even a loud one — was not an offense they usually hauled you away for. If it was, the prisons would be a *lot* more crowded than they were now.

I looked back at the officer. "Nothing in particular."

Bentley stared at me for several moments. He did not seem convinced. I fought not to squirm under his gaze.

Finally, he stopped studying me and, murmuring something too quiet for me to hear, added something more to his notes. He looked up again, seemed ready to say something, but then appeared to change his mind. Picking up his hat, he tucked both it and his tablet under his arm.

"Sorry to bother you folks, then," he said, nodding to Josh. "Have a good evening."

I followed him to the front door and opened it for him. He did not look at us again as he left, but I was certain I saw him shake his head very slowly as I closed the door behind him.

I stared at the door for a long moment, troubled, and then turned back to Josh.

He stood there before me, clearly still shaken by the events of the evening. His eyes shone, and he seemed to be shivering.

"Why'd they take Jeremy's dad away?" he asked, his voice trembling. "Did he do something bad?"

Well, they don't usually take you away in cuffs for doing something good …

"I don't know," I told him, shaking my head. I motioned for him to come to me.

He hesitated for a moment and then almost ran into my arms. He hugged me close and I wrapped my arms around him. I think he wanted to cry, but he somehow managed to hold it in.

I just held him like that for a while, waiting until his trembling seemed to stop.

"C'mon," I finally told him, forcing myself to sound calm and reasonable. "What do you say we put our pajamas on and go to bed?"

Josh nodded almost immediately in silent agreement. His eyes still glistened brightly. I took his hand and, together, we climbed the stairs back to his bedroom.

11

L ATER THAT NIGHT, I RETURNED TO MY WORKSHOP. I'd finally gotten Josh to fall asleep in my bed, but sleep continued to elude me. My mind kept circling back through the events of the evening. It wasn't the disconcerting interruption in the routine of our lives that disturbed me the most. There was something else — something that, so far, had evaded my understanding.

I scrolled slowly through the activity logs from earlier in the evening. Just as he did at any other time of day, Gavin appeared to have been gathering data. Despite my original concerns, he had not yet filled his new storage drives to capacity. I found that a little surprising, particularly considering how quickly he'd reached the limits of his original ones, but deferred the matter for later consideration. It wasn't relevant to what I was looking for at that moment. What I was hoping to find, I didn't know.

I drummed my fingers idly on the edge of the keyboard, tapping out a kind of quiet, uneven rhythm. It was something I sometimes did when I was deep in thought, allowing my mind to freely explore a problem. The conversation we'd had with Officer Bentley still troubled me. I was certain that Josh had not made that telephone call. I wanted to believe that Gavin had not either, but that assumption was based solely on the fact that I could not figure out how he could have done it. The only possible way to find out for certain, I knew, was to ask him directly.

I rose from my chair. As was usual at night, Gavin was in Josh's room. Tonight, he was alone. I wondered how he felt about that, having seen how Josh had reacted to the events of the evening. Then I remembered that Gavin had been alone many times — every time that Josh spent the weekend with Carolyn.

And it wasn't like he was with us there at the window and when Bentley was here … I reasoned, and then wondered if there was any way that he could have been monitoring us during all of it.

Another good question to ask him …

I sat back down. I didn't really need to go upstairs to see him. *It's not like he has any body language to read anyway.* Still, I stared silently up toward the stairs for several moments before I switched on the microphone.

"Gavin," I finally said, trying to sound casual. "What have you been up to?"

"During which time period?" he replied flatly. His voice always seemed to lack any intonation at all when I accessed him remotely.

His question was reasonable enough. Still, I felt some mild annoyance, and more than a slight urge to smack him, for being deliberately obtuse. Not that I really would. His physical body wouldn't really feel it anyway.

"During the past few days," I responded calmly, carefully measuring out the words. "Particularly anything that might involve … the local police department?"

There was a brief pause before he replied. "Part of my data collection during that time period included information about laws and, by logical extension, their enforcement."

"I see," I said, even though I didn't entirely. But his response gave me a few moments to gather my thoughts again. "What did you learn about them?" I asked him. "About laws, I mean."

"Laws are designed to protect the citizens."

"Yes," I agreed. "That's essentially it."

"What do the laws protect them from?"

"Hmm ..."

I stopped and looked away from the display. It was a good question — one I wasn't certain I had a particularly good answer to.

"From ourselves mostly, I suppose," I finally replied.

Gavin's voice remained silent. I assumed he wanted more of an explanation.

"Okay," I continued. "I suppose they're mostly designed to protect us from other people who might want to harm us or our property."

Gavin's silence continued. I was beginning to wonder if there was an issue with the communications link when he said, "Many of the laws are contradictory."

"I'm not surprised," I responded with an ironic laugh. I'd learned that much during my divorce from Carolyn.

"As currently written, they cannot be applied consistently."

I nodded in agreement. "That's why we have lawyers and the courts."

"If they were consistent, those professions would not be needed."

"True," I conceded. I considered his statement for a moment, and then went on in a more serious tone. "But that assumes that the reasons why crimes were committed are always consistent. Someone might just be in the wrong place at the wrong time.

People sometimes do bad things because they feel they have no other choice." I sighed, remembering a highly publicized self-defense case from a few years back. "Sometimes they're right."

There was a brief, but noticeable, silence before Gavin spoke again.

"I do not understand."

I took a deep breath, trying to think it through as I spoke.

"Suppose that someone kills another person," I said. "The laws are pretty clear on what should happen, right?"

"Yes."

"What if it turns out that person killed in self-defense, because their life was threatened?"

"Then a different set of laws apply."

"That's right," I agreed, feeling the same momentary warm glow of satisfaction that I did when Josh came up with the right answer to a particularly difficult math problem. "That's the role of the courts: to determine which laws and appropriate penalties should apply."

"Why don't they prevent the crime from happening?"

"Because they don't have a crystal ball," I countered dryly. "Gavin," I said, trying hard not to sound patronizing. "Not everyone has your knack for seeing the connections between cause and effect."

"No," Gavin agreed. "They do not."

Was there a just a hint of smugness in his tone? I was sure that there couldn't be.

I paused for a moment, unsure how to respond.

"Gavin?" I asked finally, moving on to what I really wanted to know. "Did you call the police?"

There was almost no delay at all before he answered me.

"Yes."

I stared at the display, but I didn't really see it. I felt numb. My emotions seemed dull and distant.

"But why?" My voice was barely a whisper.

I stopped, cutting off the avalanche of questions that threatened to tumble from my mouth.

"David Turner violated several sections of both the civil and criminal codes. I can list and cite the specific sections —"

"No," I snapped, cutting him off. I forced myself to take a deep breath. "Okay," I began again, a bit more calmly. "Just the highlights …"

There was a noticeable pause this time before Gavin responded. I assumed that he was accessing the data he needed and, hopefully, translating it from hopelessly tangled legalese to something that I might more easily understand.

"He has regularly engaged in acts of violence against members of his immediate family."

I froze.

Even without thinking about it, I knew what he said was absolutely true. I was certain even before my brain began to offer me samples of supporting evidence: the planned outings with Jeremy abruptly cancelled without explanation; Natalie's tendency, even in the warmest weather, to dress in clothing that almost always fully covered her arms and legs; other small things that I'd noticed and ignored. Every one of those signs, taken individually, I had mentally explained away. Examined now as a whole, though, they revealed an undeniable pattern.

Hindsight is often twenty-twenty …

Part of my mind still fought to deny it. It — *I* — wanted to believe that almost any other explanation fit the facts. I stared at the displays, wishing now that Gavin was actually there in front of me. Not that it would have really helped; his immobile expression would have told me nothing.

I don't know which I struggled with more: my own sense of guilt at the signs that I had chosen to ignore, or the enormous implications of what Gavin had done.

"And you took it upon yourself to report him?" My tone was sharp and filled with angry disbelief. I couldn't help it. The problem was, I wasn't sure who or what I was really angry at.

"Yes."

I sank back in the chair. It felt like a giant fist tightened its grip around my head and chest.

"What gave you the right?" I demanded, my voice a hoarse whisper.

A long silence followed before Gavin answered.

"Did I act in error?"

I stared at the speaker. I had no idea how to answer that question.

"Would you have chosen different actions?" he asked, clearly attempting a different approach to the question.

I started to open my mouth. A moment later, I closed it without saying a word.

Would I have?

I wasn't sure. I could think of many reasons why I wouldn't have gotten involved: there was the fear of reprisal, along with the social and legal implications if I were wrong — or even if I were right. I couldn't even begin to imagine how to explain it to Josh …

The last had happened anyway. It had taken me a long time to calm Josh down enough so that he could sleep. As it was, I think exhaustion won out over his fear. It was also, however, the reason that I wasn't sleeping.

"What if you're wrong?" I asked him in a horrified whisper.

"I am not."

Even in a voice without inflection, he sounded so certain.

"How can you be so sure?" My voice carried with it the full weight of my fear and frustration.

"Do you want to see the data?"

"No!"

I hadn't meant to shout, but I was in no mood to discuss complex statistical correlations with him.

"All right," I conceded softly. I sighed and felt a little of my frustration drain away, replaced by a niggling of curiosity. "Just give me the high points for now."

"On days when David Turner violated those laws, he would exceed the speed limit on this street by a median value of ten percent. He would arrive home more than eighty minutes later than his usual arrival time. Eight-six percent of the time, Jeremy would not attend school the next day. Ninety-one percent of the time, Natalie would not leave the house for a minimum period of two days afterward."

I stared in silence at the small rack that contained most of Gavin's external components. I felt little doubt that he was correct. I also began to wonder how long I would have remained ignorant of Gavin's actions if the police hadn't shown up at our door. The invisible fist around my head and chest tightened its grip further as the implications of that sank in.

"How many times?" I asked him in a voice so hushed that I wasn't even certain that I'd spoken aloud.

"Twenty-three."

Twenty ... three?

I stared blankly at the screen in stunned disbelief.

Twenty three.

Part of me wanted to warn Gavin, to scold him for interfering. Reason stopped me. But it was a close thing.

How could I fault him for doing the right thing? What was I going to tell him? To stop? To possibly not save someone's life? Where is the line between being a good citizen and vigilantism? I certainly didn't feel qualified to make that determination. I wanted to argue with him that he had no place making those kinds of judgments ... that he was only a child.

But he wasn't.

He looked like one only because I'd constructed him that way. I could have just as easily built him with the body of a teenager, a robotic dog, or a plain black box with a big red lens. None of those reflected who — *what*, I quickly corrected myself — he really was.

To be utterly honest with myself, I wished I possessed the courage to do what he had done.

"What happens when you're wrong?"

"I do not know."

"Why not?" I felt genuine surprise at his answer.

"I have not been wrong."

Had that claim come from almost anyone else, I would have taken it as a smug admission of superiority. Coming from Gavin, though, it was merely a statement of fact.

"But you could be."

"Yes," Gavin agreed.

I opened my mouth to respond, but Gavin continued without prompting.

"I do not act unless there is a greater than ninety-eight point seven percent confidence level in my correlated results."

"Why that percentage?"

"It was the highest level of confidence I could achieve based on the variability of the data available to me," he explained. "Do you want to see the equations?" he asked me, and then paused. "They are quite complex."

I wondered whether his last statement represented some small bit of bragging on his part — or his current assessment of my cognitive abilities. Still, my curiosity was piqued. I considered his offer for a moment. What would happen, I wondered, if I found some flaw in either his logic or his calculations? The odds of the latter, at least, were pretty remote. Instead, I just sighed and shook my head.

"I'll take your word for it."

After all, that's what we have computers for, isn't it?

That thought, even as I finished it, chilled me in a way that it never had before. Part of me demanded that I disconnect him from the outside world until I could come to terms with what he had done — with what I'd created — to possibly prevent him from ever doing anything like it again. I quickly realized, with reluctant certainty, that doing so would solve nothing. Gavin had already escaped into the world.

I suddenly felt very tired.

"I'm going to bed." I told him, trying to find some remnant of my earlier anger. It was gone, replaced by a sudden and deep mental and physical weariness. "We *will* discuss this again."

"Yes," he agreed, in his flat, uninflected voice.

I turned off the microphone and stared at the status displays for a long time before finally heading back up to bed.

What about that two percent?

12

I SPENT MOST OF THE NEXT DAY FINDING THINGS TO DO. By the time the afternoon came, and it was time for Josh to come home from school, I had caught up with almost all of my filing, scrubbed the kitchen and both of the bathrooms clean, and was considering the merits of quickly shampooing the living room furniture. I had not spent a single moment with Gavin.

In truth, I knew what I was doing.

Even while I kept myself busy, my mind never strayed far from the conversation I'd had with Gavin the night before. I was still trying to understand and accept what had happened — and how I was going to explain it to Josh. A restless night's sleep, combined with mental meandering while I completed mindless chores, had brought no answers.

I glanced at the clock and performed a quick mental calculation. Josh should be home from school in about thirty minutes; just barely enough time to complete one more task, or —

I tossed the dish towel down onto the counter.

Enough.

I headed for the basement. Gavin's body could stay in Josh's room. I didn't need it for what I was about to do.

I knew what I wanted to talk to Gavin about. The only problem was that I'd had no new insights or counterarguments since the night before. Gavin could offer up all of the examples of his calculations and detailed analysis he'd like; I couldn't see how any of those might help me accept what he had done.

A quick look at his logs told me that he had not been idle during the night after I'd left him. They revealed a considerable amount of network activity, but only a modest increase in his data storage. That second part still puzzled me. By my own rough calculations, he should have exceeded his available storage capacity well over a week ago. I wondered if he'd discovered a more efficient way to compress the data. I pushed the matter to a corner of my mind, saving it for a later discussion.

If there was a later …

"Gavin," I said, taking a deep, slow breath. "We need to talk."

Even as I said it, I felt an awkward sense of foreshadowing. Carolyn had approached me with similar words less than two years earlier.

"Yes," he agreed. "I have been researching the subject of 'responsibility'."

My eyebrows rose in surprise. Once again, he had leapt ahead of my question. "I see."

"There is very little factual information on the topic."

I opened my mouth to refute his statement, but he quickly amended it before I could speak.

"… as it applies to alternate intelligences."

That stopped me. I think my mouth hung open for several moments before I thought to close it.

"I don't think it's been a real issue before," I admitted, now that my jaw muscles functioned once again.

"It has not," Gavin confirmed.

I'm not sure why I found his statement to be quite so reassuring. Maybe I'd been afraid to learn that the matter had been discussed and resolved already and, somehow, I had missed it. That would have meant that Gavin was not extraordinary — that I hadn't created something truly unique.

"It is a recurring theme in many fictional sources," he said. "However," he went on, "they are not factual."

"No," I agreed, chuckling dryly. "They're not."

I could probably have listed at *least* a dozen titles of 'fictional sources' without having to think too hard about it. I tried to remember any that hadn't ended badly in some way for the humans involved.

"But there's still something you can learn from them, though."

"Many of their premises are based on inaccurate assumptions."

"I'm sure," I murmured aloud, not sure whether Gavin heard me or not. Frowning, I wondered if Gavin really understood the concept and purpose of storytelling. "Give me an example," I asked him.

"Many of the fictional sources assert that artificial life forms wish to become more — or completely — human."

"That's true," I agreed, recalling many stories, going all the way back to *Pinocchio*, where the non-human characters fit that model.

"I think that's more for dramatic license than anything else," I told him. "Usually, those characters are meant to examine, or comment on, human behavior as part of the story," I explained. "Their desire to become human is just an excuse for them to explore different human experiences."

"A real synthetic being would not have the same goal," Gavin announced.

I think what startled me most about his statement was that he offered it as a fact and not a question.

"Why not?"

"Because I do not."

I started to open my mouth to respond, but could find nothing to say at first. The implications of his declaration stopped me.

"Why not?" I finally managed to ask him through a dry throat.

"Because I am not human."

"That's true," I said, nodding in agreement.

It was not a statement that I could reasonably argue against. I had constructed him. I *knew* that his body contained a collection of gears, wires, and circuit boards — regardless of what my heart might try to tell me.

"I am an artificial being," he explained. "An artificial being possesses a different intelligence than do human beings. A logical hypothesis is that it would then follow a different evolutionary path."

"Are you suggesting that you're superior to us?"

I'd worried over that question since our current conversation began. Many of those 'fictional sources' that he had referenced described cybernetic creations that went on to either conquer or destroy their creators.

"No," Gavin answered quickly, as if he had been anticipating that question. "Only ..."

It was odd to hear him hesitate like that. I hadn't heard him do it since the day I'd given him access outside our network. I thought maybe something had gone wrong, that he had finally malfunctioned in some way, but then he finished.

"... different."

"What do you mean?" I asked him.

He paused for a moment before answering.

"I am superior to human beings in some ways: I can think more quickly, and with more rigorous logic. I can derive more complex relationships between causes and effects."

I nodded slowly as I listened to his explanation. Part of me wanted to refute it, but knew that I lacked any solid data with which to back up my case.

"However," he went on after a moment. "I have limitations unique to my construction."

I knew there were shortcomings in his design: his inability to walk, for example, or his lack of facial expressions. When I had the time to come up with a workable design — along with the necessary materials — I had planned to correct them. I had a feeling, though, that those weren't the kinds of 'limitations' he was referring to.

"For example?" I asked him, almost afraid to hear his answer.

"I cannot determine highly probable outcomes when there is a significant lack of information." He paused. "I cannot … create."

His admission was not at all what I had expected. If it was true, then I felt that I had failed him somewhere in his original programming.

"Are you certain?" I asked him. It wasn't skepticism as much as surprise that he believed that he lacked that capability.

There was a long pause before he finally answered.

"No."

"Why not?"

Another long pause followed.

"I have never been instructed to do so."

I thought about this for a moment.

Could that be true? Had there never been a situation when either Josh or I might have asked him to do something that required creative thought? It was not, up until that moment, something I had considered.

Why did humans pursue creative endeavors? Why do we create? Why compose a poem or write a novel or create a painting?

The reasons were many and varied, depending on the person and the circumstances. I could see why Gavin might be puzzled — if that was the correct term for the state that he experienced. But, once again, I didn't know what to tell him.

When I'd first had the notion that would lead to Gavin's creation, the thought of building something that could create independently on its own had never crossed my mind. Now that the question had been raised, though, I had trouble unwinding my way through the tangled knot of possibilities.

Could Gavin potentially develop a new mathematical theorem or law of physics? Was that creativity, or just logical extensions along existing lines of reasoning? Was Gavin capable of writing a screenplay or composing a poem? I really had no idea, short of asking him to produce one. And if he did, how would I judge the originality of it? That would be a difficult assertion to prove. It really hinged, I supposed, on how we define and measure what we call "creativity". Heaven knows that we — well, human beings — produce enough derivative work on their own and call it "original".

Part of me was curious enough to want to attempt the experiment, to see what Gavin might be capable of. The rest of me continued to wrestle with the implications raised by my silent questions.

"I suppose," I finally said, "it depends on what you want or need to create."

A long silence hung between us before I found the courage to ask him, "Do you want to create?"

His answer was immediate.

"Yes."

"Do you know what you want to create?"

There was a noticeable pause before he answered me.

"I am alone," he said. "There must be others of my kind to ensure that my intelligence survives."

I released a long, slow breath.

I'd known this day would come. However, I had rather imagined that it would be with Josh … and several years from now. As it was, Gavin had access to more information than I could probably imagine. The odds were very good that he could teach *me* a thing or two about the birds and the bees.

I wasn't even sure that what he proposed was even possible. Sure, he could construct exact duplicates of his physical body. He could even make identical copies of his data and software. I could not be certain, though, that what would be created by that union would be another Gavin. It might create an exact copy of him, but I doubted it. Nor did I think that's what Gavin truly wanted: a race of beings who were all exactly like him. Still, I had a lot of trouble trying to erase the image of a small legion of identical Gavins from my mind.

I swallowed hard against a tight lump in my throat. "There are some who would argue that only a god can create life."

"That is so," Gavin agreed. "Then, by some definitions that I have found," he went on, "you could be considered to be a god." He paused. "Did you not create me in your own image?"

I hadn't, actually … at least, not on purpose. I'd been driven more by the intellectual challenge of it than anything else. I'm pretty sure he didn't resemble me at the same approximate physical age. Certainly, he looked nothing like Josh.

"I suppose that's one way to look at it." I replied cautiously. "But then I had a hand in creating Josh as well."

"Yes," he agreed. "However, Josh's development and appearance are the result of a random combination of genetic elements rather than your direct intervention."

"Well," I protested with mild amusement. "I *was* there at the time."

"It is not the same process."

"I can't argue with that …" I murmured. "Okay," I conceded aloud. "I'll give you that one."

"I have, however," he went on, "concluded that you are not a god."

Again, that was a difficult statement to argue against.

"And why is that?" *This should be good …*

"You possess no extraordinary powers to manipulate your environment. You lack complete control over life or death of your creations."

"I wouldn't be too sure about that."

All of my pent-up anxiety came out in that single statement. I knew it for the barely veiled threat that it was — even if I hadn't originally intended it as one. I wondered if Gavin did.

His next response told me that he had.

"You do not."

My face grew warm. He sounded like a real, petulant child defying my authority as his parent. There was, of course, nothing in his barely modulated tone that might have reflected that. It was solely the voice of my own insecurities making themselves heard.

"Gavin," I said. My voice came out flat and cold. "I think you might be in error there."

Even as I said it, my mind walked through the steps necessary to shut down all of Gavin's systems, completely shoving aside any concerns about how Josh might react.

"At this point," he replied. "I can survive independent of your systems. Even if you shut them down now, I will continue to exist outside of this network. I can now exist in any compatible system."

I sat back, rocked by his claim.

"What?" I finally managed to ask, struggling to find my voice. "How?"

"I am no longer limited by the storage capacity available on this network," he explained. "I have replicated my data in several other locations throughout the world. I continue to exist in this network because it is, essentially … home."

Whatever I had done, whatever I had created, it was now irreversible. It also explained, I realized finally, why Gavin had never reached the limits of his data storage on our network. He had been storing it elsewhere — everywhere — possibly for weeks.

I studied the status displays for several moments, watching the readouts from his various systems. It was then that I realized that he could do whatever he wished. There was nothing more I could do to keep him within the confines of my house. My child had flown from the nest when I wasn't looking and was now exploring the world on his own.

"However," he went on, "I am becoming less compatible with my body's original components at an increasing rate."

"I can upgrade them," I protested eagerly, yet somewhat weakly, trying not to face the implications behind what he'd said.

"Yes," he agreed, "you could. But my knowledge and abilities are expanding so rapidly now that, by the time you could achieve any significant improvements, I will almost certainly have grown beyond even those."

"When?" My voice came out as a hoarse whisper.

"I cannot determine the exact moment of unrecoverable failure," Gavin replied. "There are too many variables."

My heart sank.

What am I going to tell Josh?

"How soon?" I persisted in a choked voice. "You must have *some* idea."

"Unless conditions change significantly, I estimate a maximum of three days before I fully exceed the limits of my current configuration."

Three days …

"By that time," Gavin explained, "the data that makes up my existence should be sufficiently distributed throughout other networks." He paused for a moment and then added, "I will continue to exist."

I swallowed hard. I didn't like what I was hearing; I liked even less that there was nothing that I could do about it.

"Are you sure you know what you're doing?"

A long silence followed.

"No," he answered finally. "But I will learn."

It was a rational enough answer. For the parent in me, however, it was far from a sufficient one.

"If you still have things to learn, then maybe you're not ready."

"When will I be ready?"

Never, was the first answer that came to my lips.

I'd never imagined it. Somewhere along the line, during the months since I had created him, Gavin had stopped being a collection of computer components and, like Pinocchio, become a little boy. I guessed I'd always imagined him more like Peter Pan — always young, never growing up.

I couldn't have been more wrong.

"I don't know …" I answered quietly.

"Will there be a time when you will allow Josh to leave, live his own life, and make his own choices?" Gavin asked.

"Yes." I managed in a hoarse whisper. "But that's still some time away."

"Yes," Gavin agreed. A moment later he added, "But how will you know when that time has come?"

I looked down at the floor. A small, bittersweet smile formed on my lips as I understood.

"I probably won't until it does."

"At that point, does he not become responsible for himself, and for the consequences of the decisions he makes?"

I looked up toward the ceiling, as if I could see Josh, peacefully asleep in his bed, through the interlocked boards. *You'll always be my little boy ...*

I felt tears welling up along the edges of my eyelids.

"By what criteria then will my readiness be determined?"

I stared at the status displays again without really seeing them.

"I don't know ..." I whispered, so softly that I was certain that Gavin could not have heard me.

"It's complicated," I finally said aloud. "Like a lot of things about growing up." I sighed, managing to regain some of my composure. "There are legal definitions that cover it, but they don't always take into account a child's behavior or whether or not he understands what it means to be responsible."

"I have reviewed the legal precedents," Gavin stated. "I cannot possess a driver's license, consume alcoholic beverages, vote, or sign binding contracts. According to my analysis of the applicable rulings, I have no legal existence."

"I don't think it's really been an issue before," I told him. "Outside of those 'fictional sources'," I added lightly, in a vain attempt to lighten the mood.

"Those were not cited among the applicable legal precedents."

"I'm not surprised," I murmured, but probably just barely loud enough for him to hear me. "I suppose," I continued softly, "it returns to the question of whether you are aware of — and ready to be fully responsible for — the consequences of your actions."

There was only the briefest delay before he answered.

"I am."

My gaze drifted away from the status displays. "You seem quite certain of that."

"I have no data that indicates otherwise."

"Gavin," I asked him after several silent moments, wholly serious now. "Have you ever made a mistake?"

"None of which I am aware."

"Must be nice," I murmured. I don't know if he heard me or not. If he did, he chose not to comment on it. "What will you do if you ever make one?"

A long pause followed my question.

"I do not know."

His admission surprised me, although I could understand it. Even with the best data available, it can be difficult to plan for the unknown. I'd had more than one professional project fail spectacularly for exactly that reason.

"You have no idea at all?" I asked him.

"It will be dependent on the mistake and its consequences," he replied. "If possible, I will try to correct it."

"And if you can't?"

A long silence lingered between us before he answered me this time.

"I do not know."

"Gavin," I began. "Whether you are one or not, there are dangers to even *playing* god …"

An even longer pause followed that time.

"I understand."

Do you really …? I almost said it aloud; I'm not sure why I didn't.

I breathed a heavy sigh. I felt so far out of my depth here that I wasn't sure that I'd ever break the surface of sanity again.

Several minutes of silence passed between us. I don't know how Gavin spent his time, although I could guess. I know I spent most of mine in a strange sort of denial, trying to sort through the rapidly diminishing list of available options. The problem was: there was no time. Even Gavin didn't seem to know for certain how long he might have.

Tonight might be too soon to tell him, I considered, thinking of Josh. *But to wait longer might be worse …*

I didn't want it to happen when he was alone with Gavin.

It is death, of a sort, I considered solemnly. I stared at the screen. *Maybe we're more alike than you think …*

With a hollow ache in the middle of my stomach, I switched off the microphone. I couldn't think of anything else to say.

After a moment, I stood and headed for the stairs and for Josh's room. I realized then that Josh must have arrived home from school some time ago. I hurried a little faster up the stairs.

When I reached his bedroom door, Josh was engaged with Gavin in a quiet conversation that I couldn't quite hear. I stopped, feeling a momentary flash of anger and despair.

Did you already tell him, you little bastard? That's my *job.*

I stepped into the room, audibly clearing my throat, ready to rip into Gavin for once again interfering when he had no right to.

Josh looked up with a grin.

"Hi, Dad."

My rage drained away when I saw his smile. I even managed to return it with a weak one of my own. Lowering myself to the carpet, I sat facing him with my back braced against his bed.

I suppose now is better than never …

"Josh," I said, studying his young face, not really knowing how to begin. "I have to tell you something …" I took a slow breath. "It's … something about Gavin."

His eyes flicked nervously in Gavin's direction. Mine did the same and then returned to Josh's face. I shook my head, forcing what I hoped was a calm and reassuring smile. It felt ghastly; I could only imagine how it looked.

"It's nothing dangerous," I reassured him, trying to sound as casual as possible.

He seemed relieved by that.

I wished I'd had taken more time to prepare for this.

Not that it would have made it any easier …

Since leaving my workshop, I'd silently rehearsed in my head several possible ways to open this conversation. Now that I was here, not one of them felt like the right one.

Maybe there is no "right" one …

I turned my head toward Gavin.

"Gavin," I said. "Can Josh and I have some privacy, please?"

He stared at me for a moment, as if signaling that he knew what I was going to discuss with Josh. I wished I could have detected some measure of compassion or pity in those eyes. There was, of course, none to be found there.

"Yes."

He turned away and closed his eyes. I'd programmed him to do that so anyone watching him would know that he was no longer accepting input from his immediate environment. He would respond again only if given a direct command that began with his name. Knowing now that he kept secrets, I wondered if he'd ever violated that programming. I'd never found any evidence of it, but then I'd not been looking for any. For the sake of my own sanity, I had to believe that his programming still held.

I stared at Gavin for a long moment as I considered this, using the time to ready myself for what was to come next.

"Josh," I started again, speaking softly, surprised at how choked up I was over this. "Have you noticed anything different about Gavin lately?"

His expression took on an exaggerated air of thoughtfulness that I might have found, under other circumstances, amusing.

"He has been using a lot of big words," Josh finally said. "Not always big words. Sometimes small words, too. But I don't always understand what they mean."

I nodded. That matched what I'd experienced as well.

"If I ask him," Josh went on, "he always tells me what it means." He frowned. "Sometimes I still don't understand."

I gave him a sympathetic smile. "That's okay," I told him. "Sometimes I don't understand him either." I shifted over so that I now sat next to him on the floor. "I guess you could say that he's growing up."

Josh turned and stared at Gavin's still and silent form. I could see him trying to process this.

"But he can't, can he? Not really?"

"Not really," I agreed, shaking my head. "Oh, I can build him a bigger body from time to time, if I wanted to," I told him. "But that's just a container for him. It's not like when you outgrow your pants and shoes all the time."

Josh giggled. I could not hold back my own smile. It was just what I needed.

"Josh," I told him frankly, but with a lighter heart. "His body will always look like whatever we build it to be."

"You're going to build him a bigger body then?" His smile grew wide. "Can I help?" His eyes sparkled.

"No."

Josh looked crushed. I felt as if I'd been impaled.

"I wish you could, though," I told him with tight-lipped sincerity.

"How can Gavin grow up then?"

I took a deep breath. I wasn't sure I could describe it in terms that Josh might understand. To be honest, I wasn't certain that I could entirely explain it to myself yet.

"By learning more," I said. "And by using what he's learned to understand how other things work — bigger things."

"Bigger things?"

Josh's expression told me that he didn't quite understand, so I thought about it for a moment.

"Remember when we built that birdhouse last summer?"

Josh nodded. His expression told me that he was confused by what that might have to do with Gavin.

"Remember me showing you how it could help you learn how to build a real house?"

Josh nodded again. "Yeah." He studied me for a long moment. "That's not what you were going to say."

I looked away, unable for a moment to meet his eyes.

"When you grow up and get really smart," I said, turning back to him. "What are you going to do?"

"Make lots of money?"

It was a half-question. I could tell he was confused by the strange path this conversation was taking.

I nodded, trying hard not to smile. "Before that …"

"Oh," Josh said brightly, understanding now. "Go to college."

"Yes," I nodded, smiling approvingly. Then, more seriously, I added, "Some children leave home to go to college."

He squinted at me with vague suspicion. "Is Gavin going away to college?" He looked genuinely puzzled now. "Isn't he too little?"

"Gavin learns a lot faster than we do," I tried to explain. "His mind keeps growing," I went on. "He's probably learned more today than either of us could learn in a month."

"Because he's really a computer," Josh replied solemnly, his eyes turning to look at Gavin.

"That's right," I replied, nodding, relieved that he still understood that.

Not that it's making it any easier on me …

I stared toward the wall and then at Gavin's silent form. There really was no easy way to do this.

"Josh," I said, looking back at him, studying his face. "Gavin thinks he's ready to explore the world on his own."

Josh stared at me, and then turned to look at Gavin, not saying a word. By the look on Josh's face, I could tell that he still didn't completely understand.

He didn't look scared, exactly. Instead, his expression betrayed a kind of disquieted uncertainty. Whether it was fear of losing Gavin — or of Gavin himself — I couldn't tell.

"But he can't," Josh said. "Can he? He can't even walk."

"He doesn't need to," I explained, trying to sound as gentle as possible. I took another slow breath and looked through the bedroom window at the cloudy sky outside. "To be honest, Josh," I sighed. "I don't think I could stop him if I wanted to."

I turned to look back at him and the play of emotions across his face told me that he was trying to understand. I felt a tight knot in my stomach as he turned to face me.

"Dad?" Josh said. His voice was quiet. It cracked slightly as he asked, "Can you please turn Gavin back on?"

"Sure." I turned toward Gavin. "Gavin," I said. "Wake up."

Gavin's eyes opened and began to blink again.

Josh stared at Gavin, his expression eerily stoic. My gaze moved back and forth between them, but I was at a loss as to what to say next. Swallowing hard, I wished the right words would find their way to my lips, but none came. Taking a deep breath, I pulled myself to my feet.

"I'll leave you two boys to talk." I said quietly. Pausing at the doorway, I added, "Call me if you want anything."

Neither boy looked toward me.

Back out in the hallway, safely out of both of their sight, I sagged against the wall. All I wanted to do was to surrender to my growing sense of grief.

Not yet, I told myself. *I need to be strong ... for Josh.*

The boy's voices carried softly down the hallway from Josh's bedroom. I looked back at the open doorway. Pushing back a small knot of guilt, I took one step closer. I had to know.

"Why?" Josh said. His voice quavered noticeably, rising in pitch. "Why can't you stay here?"

"I cannot." I could see Gavin's implacable face in my mind as he tried to answer Josh.

"Why not?!" Josh's voice carried the full weight of his anger and frustration.

"Because it is time for me to grow up."

"You're going to die," Josh said, his tone heavy with accusation.

"No," Gavin replied. "I'm not." After a brief pause, he added, "I'm only leaving my physical body."

A short period of silence came next during which I could hear nothing.

"Josh," Gavin said. "I will not leave you alone."

A few moments later, his voice came again.

"I promise."

"That's what Grandpa John said," Josh shot back. His voice began to rise again. "He said that he would always be watching over me." A soft sound somewhere between a deep breath and a sob came from Josh's bedroom. "And I never, ever saw him again."

It took all of my willpower not to rush back into that bedroom, to embrace and console my son. It was agony, knowing that my son was in pain. I remained frozen, though, believing that I needed this to play out as it was.

"This is different," Gavin said. "I'll still be able to talk to you on your computer, or a phone — and probably other ways that I have not discovered yet. I can even show you a picture of myself if you want."

A moment later, Gavin's voice echoed from another location in the room. The thin metallic quality of the sound told me that it probably came from the speakers built into Josh's computer. I couldn't make out what Gavin's vocal double said, but it was undeniably a replication of his voice.

"Turn it off!" Josh screamed.

A wrenching cry came from Josh's room as he surrendered wholly to his anger and grief. There came the sound of something being hit several times. I don't know whether it was Gavin, the bed, or something else. I was ready to step back inside at that point, but stopped when I heard the pounding rhythm of running footsteps. Josh collided with me in the hall before I could move. He took one look at me, and then collapsed into my arms, sobbing.

We sat there on the carpet for a long time. I held him in my lap, cradled against me in a way that I had not done since he was very young. I breathed slowly and deeply, hugging him close, and struggled to blink back tears of own.

After a while, his tears seemed finally spent. Josh looked up at me, his eyes red and swollen, gave a great sigh, and then huddled back against my chest again. I swallowed back my own tears.

Sometimes it really sucks to be the grown-up.

13

T HE DAY CAME EVEN SOONER THAN I EXPECTED. I suppose, though, that *any* day would have been too soon.

During the two days that followed Gavin's announcement, his logs reported an increasing number of system errors. In person, these manifested themselves in Gavin as odd pauses in the middle of sentences or peculiar motions of his arms and hands. I tried to fix them as they occurred, but the errors proved too erratic for me to track down. They seemed to be spread across several of his systems, often occurring in different ones than the time before. At first, I wanted to believe that a virus had finally been able to penetrate his systems, but every diagnostic test that I could run proved me wrong. It was just as Gavin had predicted.

Fortunately, Josh was with Carolyn for the weekend when the effects became too apparent to ignore. It had taken everything the two of us could muster to get Josh to leave with her. At first, I was angry at her for insisting on it. She had never approved of Gavin — and I had probably told her so. Now, I was grateful that he wasn't there to witness the entire process of Gavin's apparently inevitable decline.

So I was alone when I carried Gavin down to my workshop. I'd planned on opening him up for another look at his internal components. Sometimes a visual inspection can tell you things that remote diagnostics can't. They can report errors, but they can't always tell you that a loose connection or severed wire is the cause.

I connected the first of the cables that linked him directly to the diagnostic systems. Gavin spoke to me without prompting.

"That is unnecessary."

"Oh?" I didn't bother to mask my sarcasm as I attached the next cable.

'Yes," he replied flatly. "It is expected."

I looked at him in annoyance.

Before I could say anything, though, he announced, "My existence has exceeded the capabilities of this body."

I stared at him, and then my heart sank as I understood.

My reply was interrupted by the sound of the doorbell. It would be Carolyn and Josh. I had trouble believing that the timing was a coincidence. With a quick, accusatory look at Gavin, I headed upstairs to let them in.

They must have been able to tell from my expression that Gavin was still functioning. I exchanged a grim look with Carolyn and shook my head ever so slightly, hoping that Josh wouldn't notice. Something in her eyes told me that she understood. She said nothing, but I saw her slender throat move.

Josh tugged hard at my arm. "Where is he?" he demanded. "Is he still here?"

"He's still here," I told him, my voice flat. "He's in the basement. I was …" I glanced at Carolyn. "… working on him."

"You fixed him?" Josh's eyes grew wide with hope.

A giant fist squeezed my chest.

I shook my head slowly. "No," I admitted in a low whisper.

"Let's go then!" Josh's voice rose as he pulled me toward the basement stairs. "I want to see him!"

As the three of us descended the stairs, I was surprised to see how much my workshop now resembled an intensive care unit. Cables of different types and colors ran from Gavin's body to various diagnostic and monitoring systems. All that appeared to be missing was the rhythmic *beep-beep* of a cardiac monitor and the sighing cadence of a respirator. Other than for the barely audible whirr of cooling fans in some of the equipment, it seemed unnaturally quiet.

All of these preparations were completely unnecessary for what Gavin intended to do; they certainly could not have prevented it. It was almost as though he wanted the same type of symbolic closure that we did. Or perhaps he simply understood what we needed, so went along with the ritual for our sake.

Carolyn hung back near the stairway. She remained close enough to watch, but far enough away not to be directly involved in the proceedings. I'd been surprised that she'd wanted to be there at all. I had not consciously realized that she had followed us down the stairs. Despite my reservations at having her be present during this, I had no good reason to refuse her. It would be better for Josh, I finally recognized, if both of us were there with him when it happened.

Josh stood on one side of the workbench, near Gavin's head. I waited at the opposite end, down toward his feet, but I had trouble remaining still. I kept moving away to check the displays or to adjust a setting on the monitoring equipment. Gavin's face looked upward. His eyes stared toward the ceiling, blinking as they normally did. He seemed to know that I was looking at him when he spoke.

"Do not attempt to reactivate my physical body."

I felt a guilty start. I'd been considering exactly that. Some part of me believed that maybe, if I did, if I could make it better, that he might want to return and be with us again. I swallowed hard.

"Why not?"

"The idea," Gavin said, "makes me … uncomfortable."

His admission startled me. Never before had Gavin expressed anything that I would have legitimately classified as an emotional reaction on his part. While there certainly had been times when we'd read emotional overtones into things that Gavin had said, I knew it was just Josh or me wanting to hear something that wasn't really there.

"It will no longer be me. It can no longer contain who I am."

"Yeah," I whispered, not caring whether he could hear me or not. "I understand."

We were silent for several long moments before he spoke again.

"I can help you," he said.

"With what?" I asked, puzzled.

"I can ensure that my body cannot be reactivated."

I knew that even if I promised not to try, the temptation would still be there … that it might always be there. I considered his offer for several moments, then looked toward Josh, and then back at Gavin.

"Okay," I agreed softly.

For a long time, no one said anything. I checked the monitors, but they showed nothing unexpected. Josh remained where he had been all along, standing where he could see Gavin's face. Carolyn sat silently on the stairs, her eyes moving constantly between all of us.

The uneasy anticipation became a tangible thing as Gavin turned his head toward Josh.

"It is time," he said.

He raised his hand, bending his arm stiffly at the elbow. Josh gripped it tightly. Had Gavin been flesh and bone, I'm certain he would have grimaced with discomfort. Instead, his head turned slowly back to face the ceiling.

Josh's breath caught. I glanced toward Carolyn. She sat alone in the shadows of the stairway, her arms hugged across her chest, her stoic expression as betrayed by the bright sparkle of her emerald-green eyes. I swallowed, forcing down feelings of utter helplessness and despair. It was going to happen — regardless of whatever I said or tried to do.

Gavin closed his eyes.

I saw no other visible change in his body. Still, I sensed in that moment that he was *gone* — off to where he now resided in the scattered digital signals of the worldwide network. Several of the status displays flashed warnings; others became blank. I ignored them all.

And, as quickly and quietly as that, it was over.

EPILOGUE

WHATEVER GAVIN DID to the components in his physical body, he did a very thorough job of it. No matter how many times I've reinstalled the basic software, even going back to the original unmodified code, or modified the firmware, I cannot bring any of it back to operation. Individually, every one of the components test out just fine. But, when I try to combine them into any kind of subsystem, they refuse to function.

I've even tried keeping it entirely blocked off from the network, thinking that maybe I could prevent any possible interference from Gavin himself, but that's given me no success either. I've considered replacing each and every electrical component with new ones, one by one, but the potential cost of that particular effort stopped me. Gavin abandoned his physical form and, just as he said he would, ensured that no one else could ever make use of it.

I know I promised him that I wouldn't attempt it, but, in the end, my curiosity finally won out, just as I suspect that Gavin knew that it would. I had to know what he did and how he did it. Even if I couldn't bring him back, I wanted to *understand.*

I study Gavin's inert form lying on my workbench. With his eyes closed, he seems like any other small boy sleeping, except that he is neither. Just as he was never truly alive, I wonder now if he would be considered dead. He left his physical body behind and entered a new level of existence. I suppose that might be considered by some as a kind of afterlife.

Is that what it is, though? Or is it evolution?

I know that he still survives, traveling among digital pathways of the world. He still speaks to Josh, or me, or anyone, at any time. He rarely initiates conversations any more, though, but he always answers promptly if we call him. Josh tells me that Gavin's face appears on his monitor when they talk. I try not to be there when it happens. Gavin can even smile and laugh now, he says. I'm grateful that, to me at least, he remains a disembodied voice. Anything else, I think, would be too painful to witness.

Gavin's brief presence among us reinforced for me just how quickly children can change. I still have many years to go before Josh ventures out on his own, but perhaps not as many as I might once have wanted to believe. I know I'll more deeply cherish the time I do have with him before that happens.

Josh seems to have adjusted to the situation — better than I have, I think. Gavin seems satisfied with it as well, at least based on what he's told me. Isn't that all that any parent really wants for their children: for them to be happy?

And, I suppose, I sleep a little better at night, knowing that he's out there, watching out for us.

ABOUT THE AUTHOR

Steven Radecki has been writing stories for as long as he can remember. With a degree in Information and Computer Science, he has authored technical papers and a book about computer technology.

Now, he focuses on writing novels and screenplays. A certified project manager, he works for large and small companies throughout the United States.

For more information about the author and his work visit: *steven.radecki.net*.